Journey to the Gorta

Ryan McCullough

ISBN: 978-1-913275-53-2
Ebook ISBN: 978-1-913275-59-4

This book was published in cooperation with
Choice Publishing, Drogheda, Co. Louth,
Republic of Ireland.
www.choicepublishing.ie

Chapter One

Leaving Kerry Behind

Floating like a ghost across the hills of Ireland, there was nothing beneath me, but a vast green blur. I was a collection of molecules without mass, traveling at the speed of light. The friction and heat were excruciating. Suddenly, a growing sensation of weight gripped me and dragged me to the ground.

I awoke in a puddle of sweat. The warmth of the sun poked through my shuttered eyes. I jumped out of bed, slid on my clothes, and ran down the stairs. I was far too excited for coffee, and far more energized than caffeine could provide. Just one thing dominated my thoughts for days, the machines were ready, and today I would take my first ride. Anticipating the splendour of my creations, I pulled on my boots, grabbed my coat, and sprinted to the barn. It was a cool spring morning, a perfect day for the test.

Inside the barn, a shiny collection of plastic and metal beckoned me to my work bench. Years of toiling had led me to this day. My prototype was ready. It weighed 60 kg, a wearable device, although this one would be worn by my least favourite sheep. My version was much lighter; it was scaled down from the prototype, but its function was the same. Each device comprised of a computer, an argon tank, a canister of chemicals connected to an intravenous line, and a lithium battery. If my calculations were correct, it would teleport me across Ireland. The science wasn't perfect. It was more a function of energy. The power supply could send me anywhere from 100 to 200 km. The direction I'd be thrown was all I had control of. I set the coordinates on both machines and prepared for my adventure.

Dragging the heavier apparatus from the work bench, I walked into the pen, hoisted it on my sheep and tightened the straps. I inserted the intravenous line and the electrical probe into her thigh. The IV provided the chemicals needed for the trip. The electronic probe worked in concert with the argon gas, breaking her up into atoms and teleporting her in a flash. I opened the valve on the

1

argon tank, turned on the switch and stepped back. Within seconds there was a high-pitched screech from the machine, a squeal from the sheep, followed by a blinding burst of blue light. She was gone. A smell similar to burning hair lingered. It was incredible! The years spent on an implausible experiment had worked...unless I had just vaporized my sheep.

My heart pounded hard and fast. Excitement trickled through my body. My elation dwindled as reality set in. Up until this point, I hadn't considered the risk. This had been a tough year for me, all around. First, I lost my job to Covid, then my wife. It was all very depressing. The only thing keeping me from slipping deeper in despair was my continued work on the teleporters. Seeing the experiment bear fruit, alleviated my sadness and spiked my optimism. It was hard to see a down side to trying this out on myself, yet the fear of the unknown persisted.

Taking a deep breath, I backed up to the work bench, stretched my arms through the shoulder straps, and stepped forward, bearing the weight of the machine on my back. I gathered up the lines dangling along my side, and inserted the IV and the electrical probe into my wrist. There was nothing stopping me now. The argon hissed as I opened the valve. I turned on the power and my body seized up. The pain was intolerable, like an electric shock. There was a loud screech, a warm neon glow, then I blacked out.

Darkness engulfed me. A sliver moon appeared as I blinked into consciousness. How long was I out? It must have been hours. My body was in a terrible state. As my eyes adjusted, they consumed my surroundings. There were no lights near or far. Nothing but silence. Anchored by my machine, I wiggled my body to the side, disconnected the lines from my wrist and slipped my arms from the shoulder straps. It was too heavy to carry so I dragged it under a gorse bush. Pulling out my phone I snapped a picture. The GPS tag would guide me back to this spot to retrieve my machine.

My Google search for a taxi was fruitless. There was no map to follow and none of the apps seemed to work.

My first instinct was to find a road. Cloaked in darkness I stumbled down the hill a few hundred meters. It was like a drunken dance, so I waited for daylight and powered down my phone to conserve the battery. Sitting on the damp grass I relished in my success.

I jumped to my feet as the sun breached the horizon, and

continued down the slope. As the minutes passed the light unveiled my vast surroundings. There was no infrastructure, no farms, with no road in sight. All I wanted to do was share my success and return home. The excitement was overwhelming. This would be a game changer for me. My financial slump would be history and the applications for teleportation would be limitless.

Cutting through the morning mist, I resumed my search for a road. As I sipped from a creek my eye caught a blurred movement in the distance. It was a man on a horse. I screamed out but he rode off without hearing me. Continuing in the direction he was riding; I was escorted by his wake to a trail and followed it through the brush. It led to an old farmers road. Following the road, ushered me to an old stone cabin with a burned-out thatch roof. My first sign of civilization. Peeking through the only window, my eyes focused on a man curled up on the floor. He was old, frail, and eerily still.

Pushing the door open, I called out 'Hello!'

He did not reply. Stepping closer, I called out again. There was no response. He was thin, grey, and quite obviously dead. I jumped back, having never come upon a dead body before. Not knowing what to do, I powered up my phone and dialled 999. There was still no signal. Even in the most isolated areas you can make an emergency call. It didn't make sense. I stepped outside to gather myself. There was nothing I could do, so walked away briskly.

There was a familiar smell of turf burning. I lifted my head to breathe it in, and saw its smoke in the distance, and picked up my pace. Just ahead I saw a figure approaching. It was a young boy. I yelled out to him, 'Excuse me. Is there a store or a petrol station around here? Somewhere I can get some food?'

As the boy drew closer, I could see he was dirty, shoeless, and he peered at me with questioning eyes. He stared at my rubber boots with a curious look. Without lifting his gaze, he motioned with his arm. 'There's a tent down the road, with soup.'

'A tent?'

'Yes sir. Straight down the road you can't miss it.'

'Where am I?'

'Just outside of Clifden.'

I knew Clifden well. This was not it. My coordinates should have placed me around Limerick. The reality became apparent that my experiment had gone horribly wrong. It was like a treasure hunt of hints had been spilled out in front of me. The lack of infrastructure, the burned-out thatched roof. No tarmac roads. No cell service. Leaving in the morning arriving in the evening. Feeling panicked, I hunched over and gasped for air. My body was trembling uncontrollably. The boy became startled, backed away and continued past me.

'What year is this?' I yelled.

He turned and blurted, '45'. Then ran away.

I fell to my knees, realising I had not only teleported myself through space, but also through time. A terrible time for Ireland. My anxiety peaked and I broke down in tears. What was I going to do? How was I going to get back? While processing my predicament, I became increasingly distraught. Where was I going to get electricity to charge my machine? There was certainly no electricity here. Perhaps in Cork or Dublin? Did they have electricity in 1845? I couldn't even Google it. Desperation continued to pulse through my body, as I fumbled for my phone, then scrolled through my pictures. Opening the photo of my machine on the hill, I pulled up from the bottom of the screen to view the GPS tag. The image remained fixed. There was no tag. No cell towers. No satellites. I was truly lost in time. The reality of my situation was dismal. How would I find my way back to my machine and in turn, my time? This was a history I knew the conclusion of, and without resources my prospects were extremely bleak. My best-case scenario would be filled with hardship. My worst-case scenario would add me to the millions of victims. Euros had no value. They didn't exist. I needed food and transportation. I needed perspective. My negative thoughts weren't going to get me out of here. My intellect was my greatest asset. In this time, I'd be considered a genius, after all I did invent a time machine. Living in history, could be an adventure. A famine pot soup was my first step home. I pulled myself up from my knees, wiped my tears and continued down the road towards the tent.

Chapter 2

Feast or Famine?

The tent was shrouded by a disheartened line of people and I ratcheted down my pace. All eyes were upon me as they scrutinized my approach and peered at my rubber boots. They began speaking amongst themselves in Irish, a language I never managed to grasp. As I stepped closer to join the queue, they stepped back and gestured me to the front of the line. There was an instant deference, that I didn't deserve. My clothing was clean and tidy and I certainly contrasted with everyone. Rejecting their gesture and I stepped to the back of the line, and addressed the people closest to me.

'Does anyone speak English?'

A young man in his thirties stepped towards me, 'I do.'

He was thin, with mousey brown hair and a full red beard, that seemed too large for his body.

'I'm Patrick. What can I do for you?'

He gave up his place in the queue and joined me at the end.

'Hello Patrick. I'm Ryan.'

His accent was alien to me. I couldn't figure out where he was from. Perhaps it wasn't where he was from. His accent was from a time not a place. It was an interesting thought. Everyone in the queue was now facing us. Patrick was staring me up and down, with no ability to shield his curiosity.

'You from Dublin? Those are some fancy Wellingtons you have,' as he motioned to my boots and continued. 'I've never seen a coat like that before. Can I touch it?'

I was wearing a yellow and black nylon coat with a zipper concealed by a flap. I leaned forward and he began rubbing his chafed hand along my shoulder, then brushed my zipper with his fingers. He seemed awe struck, with no sense of personal space. I stepped back.

'How does this work?' I asked, as I broke his trance, 'The famine pot?'

'Famine? This is just the church helping us out with a meal. You

5

probably heard; the blight took our crops. We didn't plan for this. It's been a tough go, but it'll all be fine by next summer. If we can manage til then.'

I could only hope his optimism would carry him through what the future would unleash. Sadly, he had no idea of the deep scar that was about to cut through the island.

I realised the famine had not really hit the population yet. Famine pot was a term not yet used. The pots would not actually start getting distributed until 1847, if I remember my history correctly. If the crops here had just failed, I imagined it must be September or October 1845.

I had so many questions to ask my historic friend. I mumbled as I tried to find my words.

'What day... What's the date today?'

Patrick glanced upward, 'The 3rd.'

I stood quiet for a second then blurted out, 'September?'

He laughed, 'October... we're all wondering why a man like you, is queueing up with us? You have the fanciest clothes we've ever seen. Green Wellingtons, blue pants, your coat. You seem like someone of means.'

I was wearing blue jeans and a cheap pair of rubber boots, yet I felt out of place and just wanted to tell him the truth. I didn't know if the concept of time travel was even considered this far back. Again, I stretched my mind to think of a believable reason.

'I lost my money,' I said. 'I haven't eaten for a couple of days.'

'Well, they'll sort you out here. What line of work are you in?'

I was a computer engineer but that job didn't exist in 45.

'I'm a compu.... I'm an engineer.'

He tilted his head, 'There's no trains here, and you're a long way from Dublin. How did you get here?'

It was getting difficult to lie with every answer. Apparently, I'm a train conductor now. I could only assume there were trains in Dublin and none here.

Choosing my words carefully, I responded, 'I came by horse. I was thrown and it ran off with my money pouch.'

That seemed believable, and Patrick didn't bat an eye. We continued talking about the blight as the queue slipped inside the tent. He pushed aside the canvas curtain and we entered. It felt as though I was on a movie set. There were logs for seating, with no tables. The floor consisted of dirt and matted grass. In the centre was an iron stove with a boiling pot of soup. Beside the stove sat two wooden buckets; one half full of soup to top up the pot, the other, full of water and tin cups. The tent was warm and smelled of cabbage and the odour of hard-working people, without modern hygiene. It wasn't an unpleasant smell, it just was... a smell of the time.

I was greeted by two nuns standing in front of the only table. They froze as I stepped closer. One reached out and touched the sleeve of my coat.

'What kind of skin is that?' she asked.

I wasn't sure how to respond. I blurted out, 'It's nylon from France.'

Now, I was lying to a nun. I just wanted to eat and figure out my next move. A nun tore off pieces of soda and handed it to us. I watched as two men got up and deposited their empty tin cups into the wooden bucket, next to the stove. The other nun reached into the bucket, grabbed two cups, and proceeded to wipe her finger around the brim. She dumped the rinse water back into the bucket, ladled soup into both and handed it to us. I don't know if my face showed the shock I was feeling. I had just left a pandemic and now I'd be eating soup from the swirl of everyone in the tent. We thanked them and sat down on a log next to a group of women. Everyone was talking quietly amongst themselves. I put the bread on my lap, my cup by my side and unzipped my coat. The tent fell silent.

Patrick spoke with a half-chewed piece of bread in his mouth, 'Do it again,' he mumbled as he swallowed his bread.

'Do what?' I asked.

'Unbutton your coat with the slide button,' he said, as he gulped back some soup.

I took a bite from my bread and zipped my zipper up and down. Suddenly, all the woman around me stood up and gazed at my zipper. Everyone watched in astonishment. I zipped it up and down a few more times and they all smiled.

Patrick turned to me, 'Those are some fancy clothes Mr. Ryan.'

He continued eating, the women sat back down, and their conversation resumed. I swallowed my bread, and sipped some soup. It was as salty as the Atlantic and tingled my pallet; a plain soup with onions, cabbage and what seemed to be bits of pork. The dry soda bread paired well with it.

I felt strangely privileged to be eating such a simple meal from a bygone era. In the back of my mind, I was haunted by the thought of my time machine under the gorse bush, exposed to the elements. It was quite resistant to moisture but the prolonged rain in Ireland would take its toll.

I turned to Patrick, 'How much does a horse cost?'

A look of confusion spread across his face, 'It takes several months of work to get a horse.'

He put a value of time needed to acquire it, not a dollar value.

'How much in money?' I asked.

'I don't rightly know.'

His concept of money equated to the amount of labour involved to acquire possessions.

I continued to pry, 'How do you buy things?'

'I don't need anything.'

I couldn't help but notice his tattered shoes and his soiled worn clothes.

'What do you use for money?' I asked.

'My Da does most of the purchasing. Everything else we grow, or trade. I get some coppers from time to time for beer but lately, times have been bleak.'

'What would I need to trade for a horse?'

'That coat and your boots might get you a horse.'

That wouldn't work for me. I left in April of 2021 and now cooler weather was approaching.

Patrick revealed his hardship as we savoured our food. He lived in a small cottage with his parents, and worked the land with his father. When the crops failed, they managed to stave off eviction by giving a donkey to their landlord as payment for the winter months. It was a revelation for me. Where would I be in a week? I needed to find transportation back to my machine and take it to Dublin, then figure out how I was going to charge the battery. There was nothing of value I could trade, and there was no way I could lug my machine all the way to Dublin on foot.

We sipped our last mouthful of soup, deposited our cups in the slimy bucket of water, thanked the nuns and left. We resumed our conversation as we walked further down the road, eventually crossing a pathway that led to a cabin.

Patrick pointed, 'This is me.'

'Wait,' I said. 'I have something to show you.'

I reached into my pocket, grabbed my cell phone, and powered it up. His eyes were glued to the screen. His head bounced back suddenly as the phone chimed. A reaction you would expect to see from someone witnessing this technology for the first time. The camera was the only thing that appeared to work, but it was a spectacular device for anyone to witness in 1845. He seemed shocked and a little frightened; stepped back, but remained focused on my phone.

'What is it?' he asked with a quivering voice.

'It's a camera.'

His beard glowed orange as he stepped closer to the screen.

'A camera that rings?'

I snapped a picture of him and showed it to him. He was astonished.

'Oh, my. Oh my,' he mumbled. 'It's magic.'

I began recording, 'Say something?' He was silent, 'What's your name?'

'Patrick.'

I played the video back. He insisted I replay it repeatedly. I was mindful of the battery, but played it back one more time, then powered it down. He flinched as it chimed again. The sense of amazement that shimmered from him was like nothing I had ever seen.

'Do you think I could get a horse with this?'

He blurted out, 'Two horses!'

'Where could I find someone that would trade a horse for this?'

He thought for a second, still full of wonder as he fumbled for words, 'Our landlord is the richest person I know.'

'Where does he live?'

'I don't know where he lives. You may be able to find him down the road, he's been collecting rent for days. All the property around here belongs to him. He has two wagons and three men with him...and my donkey in tow. His name is Samuel.'

We said our goodbyes and I continued, passing several farms along the way. This would be my only hope of finding a way back to my machine and Dublin. The rain came and went. I needed to find a sheltered place to sleep. After hours of walking, daylight began to fade. There was a derelict building with a partial roof hidden by brush. I entered cautiously on the chance another body would be inside. It was empty. I found a dry spot in the corner and

I bedded down for the night, while my thoughts wandered. It was an extraordinary day. I had a conversation with someone from 176 years ago. An anthropologist's dream. An ancient meal that seemed more important than any meal I had eaten all my life. It was a great distraction. I seldom thought of the dire predicament I was in. Darkness fell, and I fell with it.

Chapter 3

An Apple for a Horse

A crash of thunder startled me awake. Curled up in my corner I wanted to check the weather, but that would be futile of course. My phone dependency became apparent to me. I longed for an email or text to fill my loneliness. What year was the zipper invented? Are Wellingtons rubber boots? Was there even rubber yet? What currency did they use? How developed was the train service or the electrical infrastructure? These were only a few questions I wanted answered.

My thoughts were bombarded by questions continually interrogating my peace of mind. I pulled my knees into my chest and huddled for warmth, until the rain fell silent, then got up and stepped outside. The sunlight was beginning to creep through the clouds as it lit up the road in front of me. My body felt stiff and hungry. Focus was the only way I would recover the 176 years I'd lost. My task for today was to find Samuel and get a horse.

Thirst overpowered me. It must have been the soup. There was a puddle of rain in the grass, I knelt, cupped my hands, and drank, then started down the road. I walked and ran for several kilometres until I came upon an old stone cabin with a sheet of canvas tied to the roof. There were 4 horses, a cow, and a donkey tied up in a broken-down shed. Two carriages were parked out front. One was a covered coach. The other full of bounty with caged chickens and burlap sacks bulging with goods. Wooden tubs overflowed with beets, parsnips, and onions. So much food.

Suddenly the cabin door sprung open, a man with a pistol shouted, 'Get away from there!'

He was of average height yet his shoulders spanned the doorway. Like most of the men I'd seen, he had a full beard.

I was startled and intimidated by his presence and squeaked out, 'I'm looking for Samuel.'

He stepped forward and a second man appeared behind him. They almost looked like twins, but he was taller, with a large knife in a sheath, hanging from his belt.

'What business do you have?' the second man asked.

I inched closer, 'I need a horse and some goods.'

They burst out laughing, 'Go on! Keep walking.'

'I have a device!' I shouted.

Again, they laughed, 'What's a device?'

'It's magical!'

A muffled voice came from within the cabin. One of the men poked his head inside then turned to me.

'You can come in.'

He moved back into the cabin. His twin thug stepped aside as I passed, and followed me in. It was warm and damp inside. The roof was charred, and the walls had blemishes of a torched eviction. Two men sat at a table eating eggs and soda bread by the fire.

'Are you Samuel?' I asked one of the men.

'No, I'm the sheriff.

Samuel turned to me, 'I'm Samuel. What business do you have?'

'I have a camera. I want to trade.'

'I don't need a camera,' he replied. A huge black moustache divided his face and appeared to connect to his ears. His eyes were branded with angry wrinkles as he chewed his food and pointed to the door. He clearly wanted me to leave. This needed to happen. I was desperate and this angry man was my only hope.

'This is a magic camera,' I cried out, then pulled it out of my pocket.

He snatched it from my hand and examined it. His finger ran across the Apple logo as if it were a fine piece of jewellery. I could see his stern expression soften as he caressed its surface and gazed at his reflection in the glass. His cruel demeanour almost cracked a smile.

'How can this be a camera?' he barked.

I reached out my hand, 'Let me show you.'

Leaning over the table next to Samuel, I turned it on. The screen lit up, a chime rang out, and all the men gasped in complete awe. Again, he grabbed it from me. He was spellbound. I reached for the phone to select the camera mode. He slapped my hand and continued to gaze at my background picture. I knew he was hooked and he hadn't even seen the camera yet. The sheriff and his two thugs stood behind him, dazzled by this spectacular device.

I figured I should ask for an unreasonable trade and work down from there, 'I want 2 horses for it.'

He answered immediately, without lifting his focus from my phone, 'I can't give you any horses. I need them for the carriages.'

I pulled the phone from his hand. He looked back at me like a sad child, 'You can have the donkey.'

The donkey would be a good start. I knew I would need more in the coming days, and this was my only tradable possession.

'I'll take the donkey, but I need provisions, some rope and a hundred.... A hundred money.'

I had no idea what the currency was. He looked at me, then back at the device in my hand. I turned on the camera, took a picture of the four men, then handed it back to him. All four of those mean bastards smiled. I leaned over, took my two fingers, and enlarged the picture. They all gasped in amazement.

'Let me show you something else.' I put it to video mode. 'Do we have a deal, Samuel?'

'The donkey and provisions. Not one pound.'

I needed money. Food would only last so long, and I needed the cash to get to Dublin. I had to build a transformer to charge my battery, and that would take tools and materials.

I laid the phone on the table in front of him, and played the video. He shuddered with excitement. They all did. It blew his mind. Without taking a breath he pulled out 2 five-pound bank notes, and tossed them on the table.

He gestured to the thug with the pistol. 'John, here will set you up with provisions. Get the donkey ready.'

I stuffed the bank notes in my pocket and started to follow John out the door.

'Don't leave,' he snapped. 'You need to show me how this works.'

I pulled up a chair and sat beside him. I casually ate pieces of the soda bread as I went through each step. He was not a quick teach. I think technology was so far from his grasp or anyone in this time. I spent half an hour instructing him, while nervously watching the battery deplete. I felt no guilt about taking all I could from this guy, after all, he did take Patrick's donkey. He was in a world of his own. Taking pictures and videos of everything. He didn't notice me getting up from the table.

'Are we good?' I asked.

'Good for what?'

'Can I go now?'

'Ya, you can go my friend.'

Now I was his friend. Well, until the battery died. I opened the door to leave, then turned to him.

'Would it be possible to get one of those chickens?'

'Of course. Just tell John.'

John and my donkey were waiting outside. It was grey with a white leg. Two burlap sacks full of food were tied together, straddled over its back and a rolled-up length of rope looped around the donkey's neck. I asked John for a chicken. He wrapped twine around its legs, then tied it to a burlap sack. He handed me the reins, and gave me a pat on the back. I began the search for my time machine.

I tried riding the donkey but kept sliding off its bare back. Grabbing its reins, I ran down the road. As soon as Samuel's cabin was out of sight, my pace picked up to a full sprint. I needed to put as much distance as possible between me and Samuel's crew, before the battery died. He had at least 2 hours of battery life left, if he kept using it. Longer if he put it away. The derelict house was a blur as I sped past it. Finally, I saw the path that led to Patrick's cottage. He was adding more thatch to his roof, saw me coming, and climbed down to greet me.

'I see you found Samuel,' he said, as he patted the donkey.

'Yes. I'm sorry I have your donkey but I need it to carry a heavy load to Dublin.'

'Don't you worry,' he said. 'It was payment from me to him, and now payment to you. Better you have it than Samuel.'

I untied the chicken and gave it to him. Forging through a burlap sack, I pulled out some onions, carrots, and beets, and set them on the ground.

He was elated, 'Thank you so much Mr. Ryan.'

'Thank you, sir,' I replied.

He invited me to stay for dinner but I had to go and left down the path.

My pace was intense. I continued in a frenzy passing the soup tent, that was closed for the morning. Eventually, I came upon the cabin with the old dead guy. I didn't dare look inside. I practiced riding the donkey until I slipped off; constantly checking for Samuel behind me. Finally, the end of the road appeared that led to the footpath, and a mountain.

Reaching into a burlap sack I grabbed a couple of carrots, took

14

a bite of one, and fed the other half to the donkey. It was sweet, wet, and juicy. I continued through a field, stopping at a stream to drink and water my beast of burden. There it was, the base of the mountain. My hopes were, this was the slope I had descended in the darkness the night I had arrived. There were clusters of gorse bush scattered on the hillside, one of them may be harbouring my time machine. Gripping the reins tightly, I began my assent and reached the first gorse bush. Tying my donkey to the bush, I resumed my search. Hours ticked away. I peered under every bush in my path. My hands were scratched and spotted with blood. When dusk rolled in, I made my way back to the donkey and the burlap sacks. It was a bitter sweet reward, as I knew this food was taken from Samuel's poor tenants. That didn't stop my hunger. There was a napkin with butter and soda bread. There were carrots, beets, onions, and some dry salted beef. I ate in the light of a partial moon and passed out.

In the morning, I cast off my pessimism, ate buttered soda bread, stretched out and inhaled the clean morning air. Today I was going to find my time machine, tie it to my donkey, and take it to Dublin. After leaving the donkey in an open patch of graze, I continued my search.

The day was full of clouds and sun. I climbed up the slope checking each bush, across and up again, in a grid like pattern. Another night was approaching and my time machine was still lost. My buoyancy sank. I took shelter under a large spruce tree and slept in the cool damp air.

Another deep breath of optimism to start my day, followed by a disappointing outcome. This played out day after day. I searched the mountain top to bottom unable to locate my time machine. It was dark the night when I arrived. The GPS tag was supposed to lead me back here. A week of continual searching turned up nothing. My machine was lost. I felt physically ill. This was going to be my life. The famine was going to make things worse. It could be a death sentence.

Sleep did not come easy. I was consumed by a sense of doom. Rain dripped down through the spruce all night. By morning my pants were wet, and my mood sombre. Today I would end my search, and head to Dublin. The famine hit hardest in the west, so heading east would offer me the best chance for survival. After loading the donkey, I began my descent. What would I do? How

15

could I prosper? In my mind, this was always a temporary trip. Like an amazing vacation in time. I'd be back to 21 in a fortnight. Now it was permanent. Adjusting to a life full of famine and anguish was inconceivable.

Chapter 4

Living in the Past

The rain was persistent and cruel. A tormenter depleting my optimism. My donkey, listened to my stories of woe with large compassionate ears. I called her Oprah. She was my sounding board, and would occasionally snort or honk as if she felt my pain. My future was set, there was nothing I could do to change it. My fantasy of building a new time machine was a pipe dream. Microchips didn't exist, nor did the technology to produce them. Up until now, I had started each day with a positive outlook. Every day was a new challenge. An adventure. A problem to conquer. Today was not one of those days.

Traversing through the rushes we came upon a mixed field of wild grass and barley. Remnants of an old farm crop. I caught site of a tangled cluster of trees, concealing a cottage within. Nudging Oprah to a trot we headed towards it. The cottage was surrounded by blackberry bushes laden with fruit. It was visibly abandoned, but not torched. Oprah found shelter under a tree. I negotiated my way through the raucous brush to the old Dutch door and stepped inside. A musky smell permeated the air, yet it was a welcomed respite from the rain.

Inside the roof was intact, but black with mould. There was a loft with a straw mattress and a blanket hanging on a line. The main living area was in good shape, with an occasional plant sprouting up through the dirt floor. It had all the comforts of home. A small table with two chairs with a porcelain cup and bowl. A fireplace with an old rusty pot. A pile of turf and wood stacked next to it. The mantle had candles and matches. This brought a smile to my face. I hadn't had a warm night in over a week and relished the idea of sitting by a fire. This proper Irish weather was getting old.

I heard something scurrying in the loft, climbed up the ladder and saw a mouse dive under the mattress. I lifted it and a dozen mice shot out in all directions. Yikes. This had to go. Over the edge and down below. I climbed down and ripped it open. It stunk of piss. I tossed several pink babies outside. The nests were dry and

17

perfect for kindling. I pulled them from the mattress, threw them into the fire place, and set them alight. A little turf and wood, and the fire was radiant. Within minutes the mattress was incinerated, and the turf and wood were burning strong.

I continued to clean and found more unembellished gifts. Some neatly folded rags, a book, cutlery, and a lamp half filled with oil. I poked my head outside. The rain had dwindled to a light mist, so I stepped out. Oprah was eating blackberries. An overflowing rain barrel and bucket sat next to the house. I filled the bucket with water, spotting a shed in the back obscured by bushes. Threading through the brush to the shed, unveiled more treasures. A sickle, a shovel, and a pitch fork. Turf and wood were stacked against one of the walls. I grabbed the sickle and cut a pathway to the cabin, feeding on blackberries along the way. It was a good feeling to have a sense of home, and a distraction. Filling my bowl with berries, I worked for hours, inside and out. I took a bucket of rain water and scrubbed the loft. The blanket smelled funky, so I took it and my rusty pot outside to the nearby stream. While the blanket soaked, I used sand and rocks and scrubbed my pot to a silver sheen; then filled it, twisted the water from my blanket and returned to my fire.

The water was clean and cold. I dipped a cup inside to fill it, then hung the pot on the trivet and straddled the blanket over two chairs by the fire. After sharpening the dull knife on a stone wall, I cut up veggies and the last of the dried beef. It was the soul food I needed to get my mind right. Once the blanket was dry, I stripped off my wet clothes and hung them by the fire. The smell of food filled my primitive home. Wrapped in a blanket, I fell asleep in the chair.

A crackle from the fire startled me awake. It was dark. I used the red embers in the fireplace to light a candle, that illuminated the room. I ladled some soup in a bowl, ate it, and passed out again.

By morning I was bridged across two chairs. Oprah was trumpeting and the crows were murdering the silence. I opened the door and shielded my eyes as the crows strobed the morning sun and flew off with small pink parcels. There was much work to do to get this place comfortable.

After finishing my lukewarm soup, I got to work. Mouse droppings littered the table, next to some half-eaten blackberries. Eradication was the task for the day. I needed to make a dead fault trap, something I'd seen on a survival show. It was a simple design using a heavy stone teetering on a carefully placed twig, that crushed the mouse when triggered. I pulled a flat rock from the stream, brought it back to the cabin and bated it.

The door and window were open to banish the stale air. I worked hard and fast attacking the brush. It didn't take long to finish the front, but it left me parched. Grabbing the soup pot, I took it to the stream and filled it with drinking water. Upon returning, my dead fall trap was triggered. I was thrilled. Who knew? I set and baited it and went back to work wiping down dust and cobwebs and stomping on anything that moved. I heard a thud.

Wow! Another dead mouse. I tossed it, set the trap, and went back to the stream. Two more flat stones and two more traps, set and baited.

I continued my work on the back of the yard. It was nice to sweat in the sun for a change. By mid-day I had exposed an old garden. More food. A head of cabbage, a couple of turnips, garlic, and a handful of potatoes untouched by blight. Such an incredible find. A few days' worth of edibles was a gift. I was already down to one sack of food.

Although I had bouts of self-pity, my hours were dominated by labour and my miniature rodent war.

As the days passed, I adapted. Each day, rain or shine I took on a trivial chore. One day I created a wall of blackberry branches in the stream, to trap the many trout that evaded me. Other days I'd gather barley, thrash it, and fill my empty sack. These were diversions from my reality. The truth was, I was frightened. How would I fit in? Would I be able to get a job in this time and build a life?

After using up my daylight, I headed down to the stream and washed up, filled my pot with water, and prepared another meal of vegetables dripping in butter. I loaded the fire and climbed up to the loft with my oil lamp and book. Original print, 'The Smuggler' by John Banim. 1831. I read by the flickering light. It was a difficult read. The vernacular was not something I could readily interpret, so I re-read sentences and paragraphs until I fell asleep.

My eyes opened to the sound of a soft thump. It frightened me. I still had visions of encountering Samuel and his posse. Such an encounter would likely come to a violent end. Of course, on the other side of the coin, I imagined his reaction when the battery died and felt I did my part to send some karma his way. It put a smile on my face. I made my way down the ladder to inspect the noise. The dead fall trap was set off. They all were. The mouse population was falling faster than the stones.

After a breakfast of berries, I escorted Oprah out to the barley field and continued my routine. The hours passed and a random cloud blotted my sun. This sparked a new task for the day. If I cleared out the wood and turf stacked in the shed, I could provide her a dry place to sleep. It started with an armful of wood, followed by an armful of turf, piled on either side of the fireplace. Under a log I spotted a small rusty tobacco tin. It rattled as I pried it opened. Coins! Gold, silver, and copper! They looked brand new. I had never seen a gold coin before, and thought, an ounce of gold is worth €1500. There were 3 in the tin, several silver, and dozens of coppers. My motivation picked up considerably and it paid off again. A bottle of whiskey. Wow! Oh, happy day. Thomond Gate Distillery, Limerick. Aged seven years. Seven years? I thought...That's 183 years to me. What an amazing concept. If I was going to be trapped in this time, I needed to venerate moments like this. Clean air, clean water, organic food, and most importantly vintage whiskey.

The wood and turf dwindled as I transferred it into the house. The mouse population dwindled as I transferred it out. I laid debris that fell from the sickle as bedding and put Oprah in for the night. I cleaned up by the stream, filled up my pot with water and went home to my whiskey.

The cork made a squeak and a pop, and I took a snort. Wow! 1845 was looking better already. It was easily the best whiskey I ever tasted. My friends and family back home would appreciate this vintage. It must have been the purity of the ingredients or the way it played out in my mind. Either way, it was a pleasure. My vegetables simmered, while I admired my can of coins, particularly the gold. A shield on one side and Queen Victoria on the other. As the light faded, I lit the oil lamp, sipped whiskey, and ate my food from the pot. It was a great day all around. After loading the fire with turf and wood I took my blanket, lamp, and book, up to the loft. A shift in my mind-set was occurring. It was an important transition if I was to maintain my sanity. Living on this farm had given me a chance to put things into perspective, but I knew my days here were numbered. My food would not last. I hadn't had protein for days, except for butter. Oprah had become a good companion, and I had no plans to eat her if necessity played out that way. My plan was to enjoy a couple more days here and head to Dublin. Once in Dublin I would seek out the power plant and dazzle them with my electrical skills, hopefully securing a good income.

I awoke well rested, and cut and thrashed barley all morning. The sun was breaking through the clouds, so I grabbed my coat and walked down to the stream. Jumping in waist deep, I stripped off my clothes, and began washing everything. Tossing my clothes on the grassy shore, I continued to meticulously scrub my body. It may be a long time before I get this opportunity again. My reflection revealed a full beard that was erased by a ripple. A trout! There was a trout trapped by my blackberry fence. I tried grabbing it with my bare hands, but it dashed up stream. Climbing ashore, I watched as the current delivered it to the edge of my fence. I ran back to the shed naked and grabbed the pitchfork, then stood on the bank and waited for my fish to align. I jabbed and missed. The trout dashed upstream and was drawn back again by the current. Another jab and I felt its weight impaled on my pitchfork. I lifted it out and danced with pleasure. It thrashed, so I ran back to the house with my skewered trophy and began cleaning it. I stoked the fire, added some wood and turf, and returned to collect my wet laundry. After hanging my clothes to dry, I loaded my pot with the last of the butter, and garlic, and hung it on the trivet. The fire was an inferno and my trout sizzled in the butter. The smell of fish and garlic was enticing. I pulled the pot from the intense heat and began eating. It was wonderful. I ate what I could. Setting the pot next to the fire to keep it warm, I read the last chapter of my book while picking at my trout until it was gone. It was good way to end my stay here. I decided I would load up my Oprah and head to Dublin in the morning.

Chapter 5

The Linen Road to Dublin

For a time traveller, I had no idea what time it was. All I could sense was, it was dark and I was rested, so it must be close to dawn. The cottage was quiet. Not even the rustle of a mouse. I crawled across the loft and felt my way down the ladder. There was a dim red glow from the fireplace. Everything else was black. I drew my hand across the mantel, found the matches and lit a candle.

Time to pack up. There was a rag to roll up the cutlery. Another rag, to fill with berries. I packed all the small items in my half empty burlap sack of vegetables. This would counterbalance the sack of barley. The can of coins was cumbersome, so I dumped them in the inside pocket of my coat with the bank notes. I went up to the loft, and rummaged around the cabin gathering everything I would need. Outside, twilight lit my way to the stream and a fresh pot of water. After feeding Oprah, I boiled some barley and had it with berries. With my stomach full, I laid the book on the table, and gave the cottage a bitter sweet goodbye. Oprah seemed eager. I loaded her up and tied the pitchfork to her back in hopes I could skewer another trout along the way. The sun was rising in the east and we went towards it with a purposeful gallop. It was frightening, exciting and a four-day trek to Dublin. Having food, and tools for survival gave me confidence. Things I lacked on my arrival.

We covered several kilometres before midday, until a forest shielded my horizon. I dismounted and we traversed through its narrow maze. Several hours passed. The harsh terrain lashed at us, as the sun was pushed out by rain. We navigated around a lough, dense bush, and rocky outcrops, finally escaping into a dark sky and a field. The forest canopy gave me some protection from the spitting murk, so we walked along its edge then set up camp for the night. The warmth of the cottage was a jealous memory, as we herded under a spruce to escape the rain. A carrot and parsnip were a far cry from my buttery garlic trout. The whiskey gave me a mouthful of warmth but I rationed the rest for the colder nights ahead. Wrapping myself in my blanket, I fell asleep.

The morning arrived with a cold overcast sky. The leaden clouds, bled their abhorrence upon me. Oprah was grazing in the field and came running when I whistled. We shared a rag of mushy berries and continued through the field. Our pace was slow. The boggy terrain pulled on every step. My boots were sucked from my feet countless times and my socks were marinated in peat. Nature had deliberately besieged our journey. My knees were aching from the wrenching mud as we dragged each step. There was an oasis ahead. A road, raised above the peat. Finally, this brutality would end. Our strength was sapped by the time we hit solid ground. Oprah was foaming at the mouth and I was hunched over trying to catch my breath. I scooped out some barley and dumped it on the ground, then took a carrot for myself. There was no sun to guide me. As I peered through the curtain of rain, a shadowy mass entered my stage. Some people pulling a cart. A family. I watched as they lumbered closer. The mother and father gazed at me with sunken envious eyes as I swallowed my food. They were likely victims of the sheriff's torch, towing their meagre possessions. Their young sons shared a pair of shoes, and hobbled as they stepped on their one bare foot. It was a sad image I had seen in history books, yet this was living, and frail. It had a smell, a sound, and a brutal reality. I was no longer a spectator to this history. They greeted me reluctantly, in Irish, as they passed.

I felt horrible as I watched Oprah finish her barley.

'Wait!' I shouted.

The father turned. I motioned him closer and dug into the bottom of my sack. I didn't have much left, but I pulled out four parsnips and an onion. By now the boys were beckoning my generosity.

The father shouted, 'Teigh!' and pointed back to the cart.

'It's OK,' I said, and waved the boys closer.

Reaching in the sack of barley, I filled their cupped hands. They began eating it right away. Utter desperation. Taking the rag from the cutlery, I filled it with barley, knotted it and handed to one of the boys.

The father was so weak but squeaked out, 'Go raibh maith agat.'

'You're welcome,' I replied.

They turned back to their cart and I followed. I reached into my inside pocket and walked over to his wife and handed her two silver coins. Shillings.

She wailed, 'Ó a dhia!' then grabbed my hand with both of hers and thanked me.

It must have been a lot of money. I wasn't sure of its value. My good deed gave me little fulfilment as I expected they would become victims of history. Perhaps this was only a prelude to the desperation I was likely to witness, or become a casualty of. We bid our good byes and continued in opposite directions.

I tried to keep a steady pace. We trudged onward until we reached a junction in the road that split to the right.
Glancing down it, I saw two figures in the distance so I continued straight. There was little food for charity and I needed it to last until I reached Dublin.

We walked for a few minutes and I watched as Oprah's ears perked sideways, then glanced behind me and saw two men a half a kilometre away coming in our direction. We continued and a minute later Oprah's ears twitched again. The men were running but stopped as soon as I turned. Now they were only a two hundred meters away. My heart raced. There was a feeling of inevitable dread. We picked up our pace and I began loosening the pitchfork from its twisted sheath, then drew it and turned. They stopped only 100 meters away.

'What do you want?'

They didn't answer and acted as if they were having a casual stroll. I turned and began running, and Oprah ran with me. When I looked back, the two men were sprinting and only ten meters behind us. There was no escaping this confrontation.

I stopped, turned, and yielded my pitchfork, 'Get back!'

They were desperate and angry with nothing to lose. Young men, thin and aggressive. I stabbed my pitchfork towards them. Oprah kicked and turned. One of the men grabbed for her reins. She reared up, on her hind legs, causing the sacks to fall and the barley to split open on the ground. She trotted up the road and disappeared in the haze. One of the men grabbed for the sacks and I stabbed the second man in the shoulder as he came at me. It wasn't deep, but he fell back, and I ran. My breath was dry and cutting. It burned as I gasped and turned to look. They were two silhouettes in the distance, scooping up the barley from the road and laughing. There was little I could do. I slipped into the bushes beside the road and watched as they walked away; then paced around the bush wheezing and shaking. The fear and panic were overwhelming. I felt empty and alone. There was no-one to call, no friends to soothe me. My situation was bleak.

I leaned on my pitchfork peering up and down the road; breathing away the minutes until my anxiety subsided. The rain stopped and the clouds gave way to the sun. It was in the west near the horizon. My road was heading south but it didn't matter anymore. My spirit was broken and defeated. How was I going to survive in this time, in these conditions? Looking north, another figure appeared, coming down the road. I stepped back in the thicket and watched as it stopped. It was Oprah eating the spilled grain. My dry lungs squeaked out a whistle and she came running like a puppy. Relief and happiness consumed me. Everything was lost but at least I had my travelling companion. She honked and snorted while I rubbed her head. We walked down the road until dark, then pulled off to the side and slept in the brush.

As dawn broke, the sound of wooden wheels on stone awakened me. There were voices, but we remained concealed. I peeked through the bushes. It was another family dragging their cart up the road. Several other people passed us in the early hours of the morning, but I was reluctant to engage and remained hidden.

Once everything was quiet, we joined the road and continued our journey. I passed a farmhouse, then another, then people. I nodded and continued. More people passed and greeted me as they did. I bid them good morning and carried on. There was the roar of rushing water. A vast river bending by the side of the road. It was dissected by a bridge. We went to its shore and satisfied our thirst. I sat on the bank and rinsed my boots and socks. My feet were wrinkled and white. We summed up our strength, scaled up the embankment, crossed the bridge and entered the town of Doonass.

Hunger overpowered me, but I had money and an appetite to satisfy. The streets were active and the people seemed stable, and bid me good morning as they passed. They failed to mask their scrutiny, first at my coat, then at my boots, yet they didn't seem to notice I was carrying a pitchfork. Shops were opening and industry showed little sign of hardship. There was a butcher, a bakery and a fruit and vegetable cart on the street. My hunger was immense. I approached the vender.

He looked at my coat and boots. 'Are you a farmer too?' he

asked, as he stared at my pitchfork.

'Not today,' I replied, while laying it on the ground next to Oprah.

There were baskets of apples, pears, and blackberries; an assortment of vegetables and potatoes. I grabbed two apples and a pear. Reaching into my pocket, I pulled out a silver shilling and handed it to him.

He looked at me, 'Do you have any coppers? I can't make change.'

I put it back in my pocket and felt for the smaller coins, presenting them to him in my hand. He picked three coppers and thanked me.

I ate the pear immediately, and fed Oprah the core. It was delicious, a taste unlike any pear I had eaten before. The apples were hard and tart, but flavourful. The smell from the bakery beckoned me, and I ventured in. It was a small shop with an oven in the back separated by a counter with three glass cases. A man greeted me as his wife toiled in the back.

'What can I get for you?' he uttered. I looked at his sparse display. There were a few loaves of wheat bread, three apple pies and a few pastries.

'I'll take one of those wheat breads, please.'

He pulled it from the glass case, placed it on the counter in front of me. 'That'll be 4 pence,' he said.

Wow. What an incredible bargain. I had a lot of money. I pulled out four pence and paid him.

'You're not from around here, are ya?' he asked.

'No. I'm from Kerry.' There was no hiding my coat.

'You're a long way from home. You working at the mill?'

'No. I just got here. I'm looking for a place to stay.'

He gestured left, 'Murphy's Pub, down the road has rooms to let.'

I thanked him, sat outside on the stoop, and shared my loaf with Oprah. I felt like a foodie, in 1845. Delicious fruit and bread to die for. Everything I ate was a delight. Normally I'd be sharing it with my friends on social media, instead of on a stoop with my donkey.

Although I never thought of staying in this town, it would give a me chance to clean up, restock and feed myself. Food was cheap.

I grabbed my pitchfork, turned left, passing several large buildings with slate roofs. They all backed out onto the River

Shannon. Reaching Murphy's pub, I tied Oprah to the rail out front, leaned my pitchfork next to her, and went inside. A large man with jet black hair, a full moustache, and a few days growth of beard greeted me. He was surrounded by a half dozen men enjoying a pint. Each one, well dressed, sporting a moustache and thick sideburns, as if they all were members of a barbershop quartet. I approached the bartender. His stature was intimidating.

'I'm looking for a room,' I whimpered.

'My wife takes care of the lodgers,' he turned his head and yelled, 'Colleen! Colleen!'

A young girl about 14 years old came out from a back room. She was small and timid.

He looked at her, and in a soft voice said, 'Mary, get your mother.'

'She's at the farm getting supplies, Da.'

'All right then, go get her.'

Mary left out the front door.

The bartender turned to me, 'She's just up the road at the farm. Would you like a pint while you wait?'

I sure did, 'Guinness if you have it.'

He poured my beer and waited for it to settle then leaned over and touched my coat with his enormous hand, 'Is that some kind of skin?'

'It's nylon from France.'

'I've never seen anything like it. Not sure about the colour, but that'll keep you dry in the rain.'

He handed me my beer. It was room temperature, but worthy of a foodie post on social media. Things like this were the pleasures that I could embrace.

'What's your name?' he asked.

'Ryan.'

'I'm Stephen,' he replied, as he reached out to shake my hand. It was like shaking an oven mitt with a tight grip. 'You work at the mill?'

'No. I'm heading to Dublin.'

We spoke for few minutes before Colleen walked in pulling a cart full of goods, with Mary following behind. She was a short stalky woman with dark hair and a pretty face.

Stephen pointed to me, 'Mr. Ryan here is looking for some lodging.'

27

She greeted me, pushed her cart to the side, and led me down a hallway to the back. We passed the kitchen and ended up in a courtyard.

She spoke fast and stern like a ruling mother. 'These are the facilities.' Then pointed to an outhouse that stood directly outside. 'There's a well here for drinking and washing.' She gestured to a rusty hand pump covered in moss. 'Then there's the river behind your lodging.'

We walked to the back of the courtyard. There was a building with three rooms on the bottom, the three above and a staircase at the end. Each unit had a small window and a wooden door. Mary stepped in front of us and opened the door to the ground floor unit at the end. We walked in and Colleen stepped to the side.

She pointed to the bed. 'This is it. You have your bed, a chair and table, your wash pot, and chamber pot.'

It was a tiny room and it smelled of the last tenant. There was a small fireplace with some left over wood and turf. The bed was messy with a bottle on the floor next to the table.

Colleen reached down, picked up the bottle and handed it to Mary and shouted. 'Take this and get the broom.'

Mary left with the bottle and Colleen continued. 'It's one shilling a week.' She corrected herself as she looked at my boots. 'It's one shilling and fi... six pence a week.'

I realised she was charging me six pence extra but it still seemed like a bargain.

'I'll take it.'

She took my money, pulled the skeleton key from the door, and handed it to me. Mary returned and started sweeping the flat stone floor.

Colleen gathered the dirty bedding and turned to Mary, 'Take this to the river and give it a wash.' Mary leaned the broom against the wall, grabbed the bundle of bedding and left.

Colleen continued with the house rules. 'There'll be no ruckus behaviour. Make sure you dump your chamber pot in the privy and not on the grounds. Mary will wash any clothes you need cleaned, but she doesn't work for free. My young Jacob is here in the morning and he'll get any wood or turf you need for the fire. It's 2 pence a bundle.'

We stepped outside. She pointed to the large apartment above the pub. 'We live right there, so we can keep an eye on all the goings on.'

'Thank you,' I said.

'You're welcome...I didn't catch your name?'

'Ryan.'

'Well mister Ryan, enjoy your stay.'

She headed back towards the bar. I cried out.

'Colleen!' She turned. 'I have a donkey out front. I need a place to keep her for a week, where she can graze.'

'For fiv... six pence more she can stay on our farm up the road. My oldest son Stephen lives there with his wife, so he'll take care of it.'

I handed her six pence.

She shouted, 'Mary! Mary!'

Mary came running.

Colleen addressed her, 'Mr. Ryan here...'

I interrupted, 'It's just Ryan.'

'Pardon?'

'Ryan is my first name.'

She seemed confused.

'My last name is McCullough'

'Oh! 'From the north.'

'My Christian name is Ryan.'

'I've never heard Ryan used as a Christian name before.'

She turned to Mary, 'Take Mr. Ryan's donkey up to the farm and have young Stephen look after him. He'll need him back in a week.'

Mary bellowed, 'But I'm still washing the sheets.'

'You can finish those when you get back.' She demanded.

We all went out front. I grabbed the pitchfork.

'Do you need a pitchfork?' I asked Colleen.

'No.'

'Free.' I said.

She snatched it from my hand and smiled. Then handed it to Mary, 'Take this too.'

I patted Oprah on the head and looked at Mary, 'Her name's Oprah.'

She chuckled and took her up the road.

Colleen looked at me, 'Your room should be ready in a couple of hours.'

I followed her back into the bar. She wheeled her cart of goods down the hall to the kitchen. I ordered another beer and had a long conversation with Stephen. He gave me a rundown of places I could get supplies. He told me about his family. His oldest son, young Stephen lived on the farm up the road. Three of his sons worked the farm but lived with him and Colleen above the pub. Mary and his youngest Jacob worked around the pub. I asked him where I could buy some clothing and he told me his brother owned a garment store in town and gave me directions. I paid for my beer and left.

Following Stephen's directions led me to the shop. Murphy's Garments. I was greeted by a small man with a trimmed beard. It was hard to believe he was related to Stephen the giant.

'Hello. Your brother Stephen sent me.'

'Ah, very good,' he replied. 'I'm Peter. Who might you be?'

'I'm Ryan.'

He shook my hand with a timid grip, 'What are you looking for?'

'A little of everything I guess.' I walked around the store. It didn't have racks of clothes, only samples I could choose from. 'Do you have pants?' I asked.

He walked me over to a few wooden frames. They were like stick mannequins made from planks. One had a linen shirt and pants draped over it. Another had wool pants and a light jumper.

He touched my coat with admiration. 'That's exceptional fabric and the stitching is flawless. Where did you find this?'

'France,' I replied.

He pointed to his stick man mannequins, 'We can make you any of these.'

I chose two pairs of pants, and shirts to go with them. Peter gave me linen underclothes to change in to. Two women came from the back with pre-cut pieces of fabric and began pinning them on me. After what seemed like an hour, I got dressed and continued shopping.

'I'm looking for a pair of boots.'

'I have some Wellington's, but they aren't as exotic as yours.' He knelt to inspect them, and looked up in amazement, 'Seamless and what is this material?'

'Vulcanised rubber,' I boasted. 'From China.'

'Exquisite!' He replied.

I followed him to the Wellington's. Finally, the mystery would be answered. What were Wellington's?

They were knee high boots made of black leather with a brown band at the top and hugged the calf; uncomfortable and expensive, even in this time. I opted for a simple black leather ankle boot, gathered a few pairs of socks, linen underwear, and linen undershirts. I chose a jumper, and went to the counter to pay. He tied all my items together with string and I paid for everything in full.

'Your pants and shirts should be ready in a fortnight.'

I couldn't wait that long. I wanted to be on the road to Dublin in a week, 'Could I get them any sooner?'

'I'll see what I can do. Check with me in a few days. I may have a pair of pants ready for ya. I only have two seamstresses and they have two orders to sew before yours.'

My father was a tailor and I couldn't understand why it would take so long. I'd learned to sew at a young age and knew how much time it took to sew a pair of pants, 'How many machines do you have?'

He looked at me with a blank expression, 'Machines?'

'Sewing machines.'

He seemed confused, 'No machine exists.'

Wow. That explains a lot. I left the shop, a little disgruntled. Not with Peter, but with the pace of things. Amazon could have delivered them in two days. Everything was a process and time didn't seem to have the same value as it did in 21.

As I continued down the street, I passed a barbershop. Well, I needed a haircut, and the experience. It was a small shop with two chairs. A young man in his 20's greeted me. He was impeccably groomed.

I removed my coat, and turned to him, 'I'd like a haircut please.'

'Certainly.'

He took my coat from my arm, hung it on a hook, and placed my bundle of clothes on a stool next to it, and directed me to the chair.

'What would you want today?' He asked.

'I want a few centimetres cut off all around.'

'Centimetres?'

'A couple of inches and my beard trimmed.'

'Shave the neck?'

'Sounds good.'

He walked over to a small cast iron stove in the corner, added some turf, and centred the kettle on top. After organising his tools, he covered me with a smock.

'You're not from around here?'

'No. I'm from Kerry.'

We talked as he cut. He commented on my coat, and my boots, and covered pretty much every topic in recent history, including the blight.

'So how did you become a barber?'

'I use to farm with my father. We had a blight a few years ago. Killed a lot of crops including my Da's. I saw a sign in the window for an apprentice and here I am. Turns out I have a knack for it.'

'Are you worried about this one? The blight?' I asked.

'No. It'll pass and be forgotten.'

I felt terrible. Should say something? What could I say? Who'd believe me? It was guilt I seemed to carry from place to place. He trimmed my beard, took the kettle from the stove, and poured hot water over a towel; wrung it out and slapped it on my neck. It was hot and soothing. He foamed up his brush and began covering my throat. I leaned back as he took his straight razor and unburdened my neck, followed by the warm towel. He shook off my smock, and brushed off my shoulders.

Staring in the mirror he calculated his services, 'That'll be seven pence.'

I paid him, and headed back to Murphy's to see if my room was ready.

When I entered the bar, Stephen bellowed a big, 'hello,' as I walked down towards the hallway, and out to the courtyard. My room was clean and tidy. Two small linen towels sat folded on the bed with a bar of soap. I stripped down to my underwear, grabbed the soap and towels, and ran behind the building. There was no one around. I took off my underwear, jumped in the cool water, washed every inch of my body, and climbed out. The towels were not much bigger than a dish rag, so I ran back to my room with them covering my privates. It felt great to be clean. I pulled the blanket from the bed, wrapped it around my body and unknotted the string around my bundle of new clothes. Shrugging off my blanket, I dressed.

New clean clothes were always a good feeling, in my time or this time. My feet hadn't been dry for days; the woollen socks rejuvenated them. The linen underwear felt fantastic against my skin. My jumper was a good fit. Roomy and warm. My new boots were snug but would loosen in the wet weather. Other than my blue jeans, I fit right in.

I went to the pub and ordered a Guinness and asked Stephen for a menu. He suggested I find an empty table and Colleen would take care of me. What choices did 1845 have to offer? The thought of having a Victorian era meal was enticing. A steak would be nice. A chicken dinner. Did they have pasta in Ireland in this time? Colleen approached me.

'Could I have a menu please?'

'Menu?'

'I want to see what you have for dinner.'

'It's stew. Unless you want cabbage and bacon. I still have some left over from earlier.'

'Is that it?'

'It comes with bread,' she replied.

That's a responsible menu I thought. One item or leftovers from lunch.

'I'll have the stew please.'

'Are you settled in?' She asked.

'Oh yes. Everything is great.'

'I also wanted to pay you for another week if that's possible?'

'Surely,' she replied with an uncomfortable look on her face. 'I'll only charge ya a shilling for next week, since I know ya now.'

All I could do was smile. She's only known me for a few hours more since this morning. I guess the free pitchfork bought me some clout.

'Thank you,' I replied. 'Oh Colleen! What about Oprah?'

She tilted her head in confusion.

'My donkey.'

'Oh. I was thinking maybe I could use her to pull my cart of goods from the farm. I'd only be using her twice a day and I wouldn't charge you a penny for boarding her.'

'That sounds fine to me.'

She ran off into the kitchen. Several minutes later Mary came out with my stew, a spoon, and some bread.

'Hello Mary.'

'Hello Mr. Ryan,' She said in a cheerful voice. 'Enjoy your food.'

33

She disappeared back into the kitchen.

I took a spoonful of stew and savoured it. Tender lamb with bits of herbs, carrots… it even had potatoes and the bread was fresh. This one hit menu wasn't too bad.

I paid for my meal and another week's rent then stood at the bar and had another Guinness. Stephen seemed less intimidating and loved a good conversation. The bar became busy at sunset. Mostly men or couples having a meal. After finishing my beer, I headed back to my room, I lit a candle, and crawled under the covers.

I was awakened by a knock on the door. It was a young boy with a cup of tea and a bowl of oats, 'Good morning, sir. Ma made this for you.'

I took it from him and set it on the table by the door, 'You must be Jacob. I was told you could get me some turf and wood for the fire.'

'Yes sir. Would you like wood or turf?'

'I'll take a bundle of each,' I said with a smile.

Jacob crossed the courtyard to a shed and filled a small cart with wood. He rolled it over, unloaded it next to the fireplace and added some small pieces for kindling, then returned for a load of turf. When he was finished, he stuck out his hand. 'That'll be four pence please.'

I gave him five, he smiled and ran off. My tea and oats were steaming. They were bland, but I wasn't about to complain. It was nice thing to do, and I finished them both.

Today I would explore Doonass. The skies were dark, so I put on my coat and rubber boots. Crowds of people walking to work, many of them went into the mill. It was a busy little town and I ventured into several shops, each time getting comments on my coat and my boots. I spent the morning picking up miscellaneous items. Things I'd need for my journey. My best find was a leather shop that sold me saddle bags. Stephen told me about the general store. They had a little of everything. I went in and bought candles, matches, a tin plate and cup, a knife in a sheath, scissors, even a toothbrush and some salt. I carried everything to the counter and the clerk began to tally up my total. I grabbed a mason jar full of honey and added it to my pile of goods. A well-dressed man entered the store and walked right up to me.

'You're the man with the fancy yellow coat,' he said.

He began circling and examining every inch of it and extended

34

his arm, 'I'm John Bindon. I own the mill down the street.'

I shook his hand, 'I'm Ryan McCullough.'

'Forgive me for asking. What is that material, and where did you get it?'

For some reason I didn't say France. I bought my coat from a sports store in Kerry. Before I could answer, a light went off in my head. 'I picked the fabric up abroad and made it myself.'

He rubbed the seams on my sleeve, 'How did you get the stitching so exact?'

I took a deep breath and just put it out there, 'I made it with a machine I built. It's a sewing machine.'

'A machine that sews,' he said. 'It's about time.'

He touched the coat all over then touched the zipper. I pulled down on the zipper tab and he was floored.

'Oh Jesus. What is that?' His face was red. He couldn't stop smiling.

'I call it a zipper.' Then zipped it up and down a few times.

He grabbed the tab and tried it himself. 'Oh ya,' he said, as he rubbed his mouth. 'I need to see your shop, and your machine that sews, and this... Zip... I think we can do some business.'

I didn't have a shop or a sewing machine or a real grasp on how a zipper was made. My father had an old singer on display in his tailor shop. I played with it every time I visited him at work as a boy. It was a simple machine with a foot treadle, and I knew every inch of it. Much easier to build than a time machine.

'I don't have a shop,' I said reluctantly. Then words started falling out of my mouth. 'My shop was in Kerry... It... It burned down. So, I came here to raise capital and start fresh.'

'Well, I think the stars have aligned, Ryan. Would you be willing to discuss some business arrangements?'

'Yes!'

'All right. Where are you staying?' he asked.

'I have a room, at Murphy's pub.'

'I know it well. We'll have something to eat. I'll come by around 7. We'll talk then. I'll be bringing my partner with me.' He zipped my zipper up and down, and left.

This was incredible. A game changer. I was ecstatic. I bought some pencils and paper, loaded my saddle bags, and headed back to my room.

Chapter 6

A Stitch in Time

This was the happiest I had been in a while. Not just here, but also back in 21. I almost forgot about the lock down, the restrictions that anchored me, and the death of my wife. I was travelling, eating in a restaurant, and conversing with people unbridled. The hardships were severe, but short lived. I was getting stronger. Like a super hero. It was a real feeling. A strength. I had the advantage of being able to predict the future, and perhaps my own. My teacher used to say, "We must know our history, so we don't repeat it." Yet, here I am. With a brisk stride and a burst of confidence, I headed back to the pub.

Stephen greeted me. 'Hello Mr. Ryan!'

'Hello Stephen. Can I get a Guinness to take to my room?'

'Certainly,' he replied.

He poured the beer and waited for it to settle. 'I see you've been doing some shopping.'

'Yes. I needed a few things. By the way, I'm meeting two gentlemen later. Can I reserve a table for three at seven tonight?'

He looked at me strangely, 'You can't take the tables out of the restaurant. What's wrong with the table in your room?'

He had no idea what I was talking about. 'Could you hold a table for me?'

'Oh...That sounds just fine, Colleen is making black pudding.'

I took the beer to my room. Odds are, I didn't have a reservation. I was also sure, I'd be having bacon and cabbage left over from lunch, for dinner.

Dumping the contents of my saddle bags on the bed, I cleared the table, and used my new knife to sharpen a pencil. I ripped the paper band binding my stack of yellow manila sheets. Not exactly the CAD, or 3D software I had become accustomed to using for my designs. Old school, to say the least. It must have been around noon, that gave me seven hours to design a workable sewing machine. It wasn't going to be easy. I used a strip of wood from a whiskey crate for a ruler, and my beer mug and coins for a compass.

As a child, I had opened my Da's old Singer many times, and I remembered it well. As a teenager, I had taken it apart twice, and reassembled it. I could visualize the arm shaft, the upright shaft, and where they linked together. The loop taker, the bobbin case, it all came back to me with surprising clarity. I visualized the mechanism of that machine in my mind, and transferred it on paper. Within a few hours, I had half a pencil, plenty of paper to start a fire, and one dirty smudged decent drawing. They didn't have erasers at the general store, although I think they existed in this time. My hands were black with lead. Real lead. Not the carbon pencils of 21. I washed my hands in the river, then made a tracing of my drawing. It looked presentable. I started labelling the parts and added a few paragraphs about its function. While I was drawing, I was rehearsing the interview in my head. I needed John and his partner to believe that I had the tenacity to go this alone. If they were to think I was going to be their competition; a competitor tooled up with sewing machines, then maybe they would pay a high price for my services.

The truth was, the famine was here. It hit hardest in the west, and the mass emigration that followed had obliterated the work force, crushing the linen industy. In 1847 it peaked. This meant, I had less than two years to make my money and head east to Dublin.

I heard Scotty returning home from work, which meant it must be past six. He oversaw a crew of bleachers at the mill, and rented the unit next to me. The man always smelled of piss and sour milk. Two key ingredients in the bleaching process. His Jack Russell terrier followed him everywhere, even to work. He was a friendly gentleman, although best at a distance.

I put on my new clothes, rolled up my drawing, and my coat, and walked to the pub. It was dimly lit with oil lamps and candles. The restaurant was crowded. I found an empty table, and put my coat and drawing on the chair beside me.

Mary came by and greeted me. 'Hello Mr. Ryan, can I get you anything?'

'I'll have a Guinness please.'

She returned with my beer.

'There'll be two other people joining me for dinner.'

'Well,' she said. 'We have some delicious black pudding tonight. My Ma's speciality.'

I sighed, 'Do you have any bacon and cabbage left over from lunch? I thought I might give it a try.'

'No, I just served the last of it.' She gestured to a table of four next to me. Three of them were eating bacon and cabbage.

'OK great.' Which really meant, yikes. I tried black pudding as a child and it was a sad memory. Long story short, I broke my granny's heart and haven't had it since. I can't imagine pig's blood, in a time before refrigeration, would make it any more appealing.

'Well, Mary, I'll wait for my guests and we'll all have some when they arrive.'

Nursing my beer, I scanned the room as I waited. The pub had a strange ambiance at night. The fireplace gave off a soft orange glow. The oil lamps hung from above, and cast their light downward, masking the imperfections of the ceiling. The furniture was old and simple. People were chatting, laughing, and enjoying themselves. It felt like a living museum.

The pub door opened, and John stepped in, followed by a clean-shaven man with dark wavy hair. I raised my arm, he nodded, and they approached my table.

John reached out his hand and shook mine. He turned and presented his friend, 'This is my partner, Robert Feeney.'

We shook hands and sat down. Mary came and took our drink order. A whiskey for John, and a Guinness for Robert and I.

John kicked off the conversation, 'Did you bring your coat?'

I pulled it from the chair, unrolled it, and handed it to Robert. He drew his hand across the nylon, plucked at the seams with his thumbnail, and looked at me much the same way everyone from this century did when they saw my coat.

'Remarkable,' he said. 'John told me you made this with a sewing machine.'

'Yes,' I replied.

'This fabric is like waxed cloth with no residue. Where did you get it?'

'I got it abroad.'

Mary placed our drinks on the table.

Robert got out of his chair. 'Can I try it on?'

I nodded. He examined the lining then slipped it on.

John reached over and grabbed the zipper tab. 'Look at this,' he said, as he tugged on it. The zipper wasn't engaged with the other half, so I got up and squatted between their chairs, then grabbed the zipper tab and zipped it up for him.

'What an extraordinary coat,' he said, as he played with the zipper. 'It's the most perfect garment I've ever seen. How long did it take you to make it?'

I searched my memory. My Da could make a shirt from a pattern in four or five hours. I figured a coat with lining and zippered pockets may take, 'Two days.'

Both men were speechless, then spoke simultaneously. 'We would like you to work for us.'

'Well, I appreciate your offer, but if I go with this on my own, I'll be a rich man in a year or two.'

Robert examined every inch of the coat.

John continued, 'You will need tools, a workshop, and skilled labour. We have a shop and a crew on site; a blacksmith and forger, who build the parts for our looms. These relationships would take you months, or years to cultivate. If you work for us, you'll be able to start building your sewing machines tomorrow.'

I had rehearsed a long-drawn-out sales pitch in my head, but thought I'd be better off listening.

Robert interrupted. 'We are aware of your potential, and what sewing machines will do for production. We discussed a wage for you and bonuses. Perhaps even profit sharing. My access to the retail market has taken me years to develop. Making a product rapidly will be of no use to you, if you don't have a market to trade in.'

After a brief discussion they agreed to pay me £50 a month until I built the first working sewing machine, then double my wage. They also agreed to profit share if production exceeded the number of units they currently produced. I couldn't have asked for a better arrangement. It was an enormous sum of money. Having access to a team of workers would be incredible. I would be able to produce the first sewing machine in two or three months. Time was critical.

We shook hands and Robert pulled out a contract. He took a fountain pen and added £50 in the blank space. My guess was they were planning to pay me less. I signed the contract, then revealed the plans I had drawn up. Robert was particularly interested in this new technology. He had thirst for it. We discussed the mill and the linen factory.

John was the sole owner of the mill. Robert was partners with

John at Feeney's Linens. He would take the linen that was produced at the mill, and turn it into clothing and other products in his factory. Robert ran the linen factory and I'd be working with him. I was so excited. The money was exceptional, but the challenge had just as much appeal.

Mary approached the table. John addressed her. 'We'll have another round of drinks, and what's on the menu for today?'

'Black pudding,' she replied.

'Splendid! Three of those.'

I went over the plans with John and Robert. It wasn't hard to tell that this was a game changer for them. One machine would improve productivity 5-fold. Thirty-five machines would make us all rich. We continued discussing my role in the operation. I would be designing and building the sewing machines with Robert and his crew. What I really needed was my 3D printer. Instead, I'd be using wood and clay to replicate the components of the sewing machine, which would be cast in metal by the forger. The smaller parts would be machined from steel by my crew. We were all excited to get started, and we seemed to hit it off well.

Mary approached with our meals. The dreaded black pudding. Such an appropriate name.

'Ah, thank you Mary,' I said, as I looked vacantly at the dark cylinder on my plate.

'Enjoy, this is my Ma's speciality.'

John and Robert dug right in. I drifted back to my granny's tears. I laid a napkin on my lap, cut off a large piece, stabbed it with my fork, and dropped it on my napkin when nobody was looking. I ate the vegetables, jabbed another piece, dropped it on my lap, with no real plan of how I was to dispose of it. Scotty came in. I casually dropped a chunk of this swine oat mix on the ground. Jack was on it in a second. He barely chewed it. That little Jack Russell had a big appetite. I pet him with one hand while continuing to dump the rest on the ground. It was a relief to say the least. I had become quite fond of the Murphys and didn't want to hurt Colleen's feelings, or relive my granny's black pudding sorrow.

I leaned back and rubbed my stomach. John, wiped his mouth, and ordered three whiskeys for a toast.

We discussed the possibilities of sewing by machine, and I introduced them to the concept of assembly lines. They were intrigued. Mary placed the drinks on the table, and we each grabbed a glass and raised it.

'To a prosperous future,' John said.

We clinked glasses, and I smirked at the irony, then we drank our whiskey in one gulp.

John raised his hand to attract Mary, put his glass on the table, and said, 'Eight in the morning gentleman.' We shook hands, John paid the bill and they left.

I went back to my room. Tears of happiness flowed down my cheeks. Having a job like this ensured my survival, and alleviated my sense of doom. 50£ was almost 20 years rent at Murphy's. My future now was hopeful, and I slept with a strong sense of security.

It was still dark, but I could hear Scotty letting Jack out for a pee. He worked at eight, so I knew it was time for me to get ready. I walked up to Feeney's Linens. It was a large building with a warehouse next it. There were candles burning inside, but the doors were locked. I stood outside and waited. Robert showed up and let me in.

'Good morning, Robert,' I said.

'Good morning, Ryan. Are you ready to produce great things?'

'You bet. Can I get a tour?'

He was excited as we toured the building. There were enormous tables for producing sails, and small tables for items like diapers. I heard women's voices coming from a room in the back.

He unbolted the door. 'This is where our seamstresses live. We have 15 that stay on the premises, and 20 more that don't,' he boasted with pride.

I was shocked. Sweatshops have a long history. We continued the tour. Spools of linen hung on the walls from chains. There was no machinery, everything was done by hand. A doorway led us out to a warehouse, an open space with a high ceiling. On one side, there were several spools of linen stacked to the rafters. The other side full of wooden crates, packed with clothing, sheets, and other finished products. We exited the warehouse, and entered a workshop.

'We'll be constructing our sewing machines here,' Robert said as, he introduced me to the foreman Matthew.

'This is Ryan, the man with the sewing machine,' he said.

'Hello Matthew.'

'Call me Matt,' he said.

It was dark inside the shop. Matt opened the large door and the rising sun illuminated the space. The ceiling was high with pulleys hanging from the beams. There were work benches, hand tools and a lathe. The lathe caught my eye. It had the identical treadle and belt system that a sewing machine had. This mechanism, would simplify the build, it was the foot propelled motor that attached to the sewing machine and acted as a table. We could simply, take this base, and attach the sewing machine on top.

I turned to Matt. 'Where did you get the lathe?'

'Our blacksmith, Garth built it.'

If the blacksmith built this, then he would be able to cast identical bases saving us weeks of design. With the foot treadle mechanism already available, we would only need to focus on the sewing machine itself.

Robert continued our tour. We passed some bleaching ponds with groups of men working. They stretched out for acres. The smell was piercing, and followed us as we entered the mill.

It was a substantial building, with several large looms connected to belts, driven by the water wheels in the River Shannon. They were weaving large swathes of linen, 100 meters long. Twenty spinning Jenny's whirled miles of thread. Over 200 workers laboured in the mill. John was across the building enthralled in his duties and didn't notice us as we left.

Our final stop was the blacksmith, a half a kilometre up the road. Steel tools and farm equipment cluttered the shop. Garth laid down his hammer to greet us. He was an older man with a grey beard and a strong right arm. An intense heat and roar came from the rear. We moved to the back where his two sons were pouring bronze casts into sand moulds and watched the molten metal flow. We discussed the parts Garth would cast for us, without revealing what they would be used for.

There were many reasons to be secretive. Robert had told me a story about a Frenchman, who built several sewing machines some years back, to make uniforms for the military. A mob of tailors stormed his building and burned it down, with him still in it. They feared it would eliminate their livelihoods. That technology remained stagnant until now. Wow! I thought. These are some tough ass tailors. Aside from vigilante tailors, we also had to worry about other manufacturers stealing our ideas before we filed for a patent. I wasn't exactly sure when Singer patented his first sewing machine, but I did know it was some time in the 1800s, and the clock was ticking. According to Robert, hand cranked sewing machines were made for leather and canvas. They were slow, and would not infringe on our patent rights. We bid our goodbyes to Garth and returned to the work shop. Now that all my introductions were made, I was eager to get to work.

After seeing the availability of materials and services, I was certain we could produce a sewing machine in half the time I originally thought. To avoid downtime, I suggested we start building three at once. Robert was an ambitious man and agreed wholeheartedly. We discussed the project with Matt and reviewed the plans. Matt gave his apprentices instructions, then headed to the blacksmith shop to arrange to have the bases, treadle, and linkage made. Exact copies of the lathe base. Robert and I worked on the lathe making wooden pulleys, and a spindle that would later be cast in bronze and steel. Working with such primitive tools was a satisfying process. You got to touch and feel what you were creating throughout the entire build, something lost with 3D printing. We worked all day without breaking for lunch. I went home happy. It was a great first day. I swung by Murphy's Garments and picked up my first pair of pants. I could finally get my jeans washed. Everything was falling into place.

The next morning, I woke up invigorated, dressed in all new clothing, and headed off to work. Robert began putting the finishing touches on the pulleys. Matt and his apprentices were carving precision parts out of wood. I began shaping the cover out of clay that would later be cast in iron. Robert and I worked side by side all morning.

By midday, we headed to Murphy's for lunch. The restaurant was busy. Colleen and Mary were running around, frantically serving the customers. Stephen stepped up to help clear tables and deliver drinks. We had a beer and ordered our food, and talked while we waited.

'I'm astonished how fast this is coming together,' said Robert.

'I wasn't sure we'd be able to work this quickly using these tools,' I replied.

He seemed perplexed. 'We're using the most modern equipment available. What kind of tools did you use?'

'I...I...used more primitive tools and wasn't sure I could adapt to these,' I said, as I tried to cover my error.

'Well, you seemed to have adapted to these modern tools quite readily.'

'You've been a good teacher, and I couldn't have asked for a better business partner,' I said.

Colleen's timing couldn't have been better. She dropped our food on the table, and left out the front door. I had to be mindful of the century I was living in. Robert would never be able to conceive time travel as a possibility. It was only my second shift, but it was exhilarating. I think I brought a level of excitement to Robert's work day. He was intrigued about the future. Not just for his company but also where technology would take us. I couldn't have predicted a better life, in a time of turmoil.

Colleen returned and greeted us. Her arms were full of goods, and she disappeared into the kitchen. We had finished our meal and waited patiently to pay. I was facing the door when a man burst in. He looked right at me. It was Samuel. His mouth twitched, much like a cat looking at a bird through a window. I froze. His eyes shifted around the pub.

'Whose donkey is that?' he shouted.

My heart felt like it was pounding through my chest. He didn't recognise me. My beard and clothing. I blended right in. I tried to mask my fright.

He repeated himself. 'Whose donkey is that?'

Just then Colleen came out of the kitchen, 'That donkey belongs to...' She glanced my way. I shifted my eyes and remained frozen.

'That donkey belongs to me,' she continued, then escorted Samuel outside. She glanced back at me, and resumed her conversation with Samuel. I could hear her raise her voice and Samuel was just as loud. I was petrified and Robert could see my distraction as I took a deep breath to calm myself.

I heard Samuel say, 'White leg.'

Then Colleen would raise her voice. 'I paid for it!'

Feck! Oprah and her white leg. The arguing stopped, and Colleen returned with another arm full of supplies. She gave me a stern look, and proceeded to the kitchen. We paid Mary and left. I kept looking over my shoulder on the short walk to the workshop and remained distracted for the rest of the day.

When I came home, I was tempted to take the alleyway next to the pub, that led to my room, and avoid Colleen. Reluctantly, I entered.

'Hello Mr. Ryan.' Stephen said, in his usual cheerful voice.

'Colleen would like to have a word with you. She's in the kitchen.'

Walking down the hall to the kitchen, I felt like young boy, about to be scolded by his mother.

'Hello Colleen,' I whimpered.

She was preparing food, and turned. 'Well, Mr. Ryan, I don't know what business you had with that man...'

I tried to speak, 'He's um...'

'I know who he is. He comes in from Galway and sells off the goods he takes from his tenants. He's a sorry excuse for a man. You best keep away from him.'

'I'm sorry about that,' I said in feeble tone.

'No need to apologise. Just don't be doing any dealings with him. It'll bring you nothing but grief.'

It was too late for that. I left the kitchen and went to my room. The whole ordeal was unnerving, and I would need to be vigilant.

The next day while dressing for work, I was mindful to wear nothing but period clothing. No coat or my rubber boots, in case Samuel was lingering in town. Galway was several hours by horse and carriage so I hoped that his visits were infrequent.

As days passed into weeks, I hadn't seen Samuel. I was calm and focused on the build. Robert and I followed the same routine daily. We would work all morning, have lunch at Murphy's, and work until dark. Often past midnight. Garth would make a sand mould, from our wooden parts, and cast them in steel, bronze, or brass. When he completed the parts, we added them to the assembly. Our sewing machines were coming together rapidly.

There was little down time, but I did manage to start on the zippers. I removed the pocket zipper from my coat, dismantled it, and had Garth cast the tabs and teeth in brass. John and Robert drew up a contract for the zippers. It was the same deal we made with the sewing machine. I'd draw up the plans and in return they would file the paperwork through their lawyer, with the court of chancery. The patent office of the time. They financed the manufacturing and we'd split the future royalties evenly. My life in 1845 far exceeded the grim outcome I had predicted two months ago. We had accomplished so much in such a short period of time, even with primitive tools. My team took pride in their work and produced flawless components. Weeks of work were coming to an end. I finished my day excited anticipating tomorrow's shift.

I awakened to pouring rain, but that wasn't going to sour my mood. We would be receiving the final parts and completing our first machine. Matt and Robert were as excited as I was. We all had invested our heart and soul into this, and we were thrilled to see it come together. Garth's son Brett, arrived with the parts and we started assembling them right away, focusing on one machine. It took hours to fit and refit the parts. Two of the apprentices left, and we continued into the night. Finally, we gave it a dry run and everything moved in unison. I slapped on the cover plate, carried it into the linen shop, and lit an oil lamp. Robert filled the bobbin with thread, and set the spool in place. Matt cut a strip of linen, folded it in half, and handed it to me. I tucked it under the needle plate and ran it through in seconds, cut the thread, then handed it back to Robert. He was stunned, and excited. Matt tugged at the seam. It was perfect. I showed him how it worked backwards and forwards to prevent unravelling, and he just beamed. We were all excited, but exhausted, and went home. Tomorrow we could start fresh and continue assembling the parts of the other sewing machines.

I was psyched. It was so late the pub was closed. I went down the side alley, inserted my key into the lock, opened the door, and unzipped my coat. I was hit in the back of my head and fell to the floor. I got up and was arm locked from behind, then punched in the stomach. I wanted to scream for help but couldn't breathe. A match lit my candle and Samuel's evil face illuminated. He punched me again and winded me. His thug held me tight while the other one ransacked my room. They found my bank notes, £55. Samuel grabbed the money, put it in his pocket, then punched me in the face and chest continually until I went limp.

'Take his coat!' he yelled.

The thug released me, yanked my coat from my arms, and I fell to the floor. A dog ran in barking and Scotty broke a whisky bottle over the head of one of the thugs. He turned around, shook off the glass and punched Scotty square in the face, knocking him out. He laid on the stoop with Jack barking at his side.

'Not so smart now, are ya camera boy?' Samuel shouted, and kicked me in the face. The other two thugs began kicking me all over. I was barely conscious. I tightened up into a ball, and knew it was over. Suddenly, an arm reached in the doorway, dragging Samuel out to the stoop, hitting him, and knocking him to the ground. It was Stephen. He punched another guy and knocked him into the fire place. The next thug pulled out his gun. Stephen grabbed it before he could let off a shot and pistol whipped him.

I could hear Colleen crying, 'Oh Scotty! Oh Scotty!'

Stephen pointed the gun at the two men, and they got up and ran off. Samuel followed them with my coat and money. Colleen ran into my room with a kitchen knife in her hand; with Mary, Jacob and her other three sons I rarely saw, trailing behind her. Mary was crying, 'Oh Mr. Ryan! Oh Mr. Ryan! Don't die.'

The room began spinning and I blacked out.

Chapter 7

Down Time

I awoke in a hospital with an IV line in my arm. I felt no pain. Neon lights flickered on the ceiling, an electronic monitor beeped, and a television was mounted on the wall. Everything was clean and tidy. The entire ordeal was a dream. I was elated. The past felt so real, the people, the smells, the pain. A nurse came in to check on me. I was beaming.

'Why am I here?' I asked.

'Covid. You had a bad case of Covid. You've been in a coma.'

'How long? How long have I been out?'

'About two months. We almost lost you.'

It felt great to be back in my time. What an extraordinary dream. I started feeling wet around my mouth and chin; wiping it with my hand to see if there was blood. The room went dark.

I could hear a nurse calling. 'Ryan, you need to drink something.'

Excruciating pain engulfed my entire body. I couldn't open my eyes. They stung when I touched them. I could hear a voice, 'Drink some of this.'

I tried to sit up but the immense agony anchored me to my bed. My mouth was dry and swollen, and my lips guzzled from the cup.

'There you go. Drink up,' she said. 'Get me the towel.'

I felt a cold rough cloth lacerate my skin, I reached up to block it.

'Welcome back to the living. You gave us all a fright Mr. Ryan.'

Feck!

My eyes were swollen shut, my mouth and cheeks bulged. I touched my face, it burned, and felt like minced meat. I struggled to breathe as the air pierced my lungs. My shoulder, my chest, my legs all throbbed. Not one part of me had escaped Samuel's torture. I blacked out.

A cold steel blade cut through my bulging eye and warm fluid streamed down my cheek. A sharp piercing, and the other cheek became saturated. I could see the blurred image of a man. A doctor.

He leaned me forward, straddled behind me on the bed, cupped my elbow in his hands, and wrenched it to my chest. I heard my collar bone pop back in. My eyes bled tears as the pain travelled from my shoulder to my ear. He stepped in front cutting me on my arm and leg. I could feel a tightness release. The sound of metal tongs on glass clanged, and I felt a slimy mass on my face, then another. A witch doctor? After several minutes my face and body were covered with leeches. I could hear them sucking ferociously on my cheek. It felt unusually tranquil.

He barely spoke. Quietly murmuring, 'Breathe. Can you feel that?' He would hum and awe, while examining my body systematically from top to bottom. It put me in a meditative state. My pain had greatly diminished. He sat in my chair and waited, occasionally wiping my wounds.

There was a prick and a stitch where he lanced my eyes, arm, and leg, then sewed up my gashes. He bandaged me up, took my pulse, put his hand on my forehead, then listened to my chest through a wooden and brass tube. His tongs grabbed the fattened leeches and put them in the jar. He snapped the clasp on his medical bag. Standing above me, putting his hand behind my back, he leaned me forward and held a small bottle to my lips.

'Sip,' he said.

I took a mouthful of his bitter serum.

'Take this when the pain gets intense.' He put the bottle on the table next to my bed.

He proceeded to rifle through a laundry list of my wounds; broken ribs, dislocated collar bone, cracked jaw bone, a chipped tooth, to name a few.

'Stay in bed,' he demanded. 'Drink lots of fluids. You should be back to normal in a month or so.'

I thanked him and he left. My body began to feel numb and warm, and I fell asleep.

When I woke up, Robert was sitting in the chair sipping a Guinness.

'How are you feeling?'

'It only hurts when I'm conscious,' I replied. 'How do I look?'

'You look like shite!'

I laughed and my ribs throbbed. 'Sorry I missed work yesterday, I really wanted to be there to teach the girls how to use it.'

'It's been two days my friend,' he said with a smile. 'I

49

remembered what you showed me, reversing the stitch, and I showed our head seamstress Audrey how it was done. She's teaching the rest of the women. It's pretty exciting.'

'Wow, that's great, I wish I could have been there,' I said with regret. 'Maybe in a couple of days I'll be ready to come back.'

Robert smiled, 'You'll need more time than that. You're a real fright. I don't want you scaring my ladies away. Don't worry, it's all coming together and you need to heal.'

He finished his beer and raised his glass, 'I'm going to get one more. Would you like one?'

I picked up my bottle of serum and squinted at the label, 'I'm OK, I'm just going to sip my bottle of, Heroin?'

Robert left for a refill and I stared at the bottle. Wow! Two days in and out of consciousness.

He returned with his pint and continued. 'John and I came to see you yesterday. We both were stunned at the level of brutality those bastards inflicted on you.'

'I think they would have killed me if Stephen hadn't stepped in.'

'John's doctor is the best in town. You look much better today.' He paused and smiled, 'You were even talking about work in your unconscious state yesterday.'

'What did I say?'

'You were talking about a tie machine,' he said. 'Linen ties could be a trend. We're fortunate to have you and your new ideas, you're always thinking. It's going to be a great year for all of us.'

'It can't get worse,' I sighed.

'Matt and I should have a second machine completed tomorrow, and the third, by the beginning of next week.
Matt's helping Garth at the foundry to speed up production for another fifteen machines. We're assembling them in batches of three.'

Robert finished his beer and left. I sipped some heroin. Stephen's middle son Adam came in, and started my fire. He had been coming every night since my beat down and would light it and leave. Every morning, Jacob brought me tea and oatmeal. I'd have it with honey. I couldn't eat solid food. Mary would come by and dump my chamber pot, bring me fresh water, and tend my wounds. Colleen prepared my lunch and dinner; mashed up vegetables and finely diced meat. I was lucky to find such a decent group of people in a time of need. Even Scotty popped his head in every day after work to see how I was doing. His nose was broken, but he assured me it wasn't the first time. My body was broken, but my heart was full. Robert would visit daily to discuss the progress in shop. He even brought me apple sauce. Colleen always had her plate full, but found time to prepare my food and share a kind word. Mary had cleaned my room and washed all my clothing. Everybody did so much… I wasn't sure how I could ever repay such kindness.

As the days passed, I got my strength back. The heroin was potent, so I only took it the first few days and tried to bear the pain. It hurt to chew. I just swallowed all my mashed food. On day four of my recovery, I entered the pub before it opened.

Stephen smiled, 'There's the scrapper.'

'More like scrap,' I replied. 'I just wanted to thank you for saving my life.'

'Ah,' he said modestly. 'You could have handled them.'

He reached under the bar and grabbed the pistol, 'I got a pistol for my trouble. Good to see ya on your feet again. You'll be eating solid in a week.'

I smiled, nodded, went back to my room, read an old newspaper, and tried to pass the time.

The days eked by slowly and I was getting restless. Colleen removed my stitches. I started sketching a button foot to use on the sewing machines, since the zipper was a long way off. It took far too long to manufacture. I needed to make them differently. Faster.

Having all this time on my hands gave me too many hours to get lost in thought. Sometimes, I would think obscure things like, Marty McFly, from the movie, erasing his family by changing one thing in the past. I surely would have wiped out my family if it were true. Perhaps the entire county. It was a funny thought. I mused about the history I'm changing right now. Mr. Singer will die unknown and Mr. Zipper too… if that's his name. What if I could go back to 21 and come back again? Would I be able to prevent the famine? Return with a remedy for the blight, or inflict political change that facilitated it in the first place. I would imagine what Ireland might look like today. Would those decimated industries still be thriving without the exodus? Would the rest of the world know us as well as they do, had we not spilled out in great numbers around the globe? I would lay in bed thinking, why do time travellers in movies never return with gold, or whiskey, or dinosaur eggs? These thoughts would keep me up at night.

Each day my health improved. I walked up and down the river for exercise, then started helping Stephen set up the pub in the morning. When I returned to my room, I'd sketch, and try to figure out how to reproduce a zipper faster.

Today Garth came to visit, 'You're faring well,' he said, as he sat on the edge of my bed.

'I'm better than I was.'

'When Matt came to see you last week he described a grimmer site, you must be healing quickly.'

I looked back at him as I sketched at the table.

'You're still at it I see. A new invention?'

'It's an old one,' I replied. After working with Garth, we built a trust, and revealed our sewing machine in strict confidence. Our patents were pending. 'It's the zipper. I can't assemble it very quickly. After you cast the teeth, it takes considerable time to crimp them onto the cloth tape.'

'I don't cast the teeth. I constructed a die from iron, with a piston and a cutter.'

He leaned over my shoulder, took a sheet of paper, and sketched out his die. It was simple, yet fast and effective. He would feed a brass ribbon into it, hit a piston with a hammer that cut and shaped the zipper tooth.

'Could we mechanize it?' I asked.

'I suppose we could, but you'll need more force than a treadle to hammer the piston. If you hooked it up to a mill wheel, that will give you the impact you'd need.'

I had been looking at it all wrong. The zipper wasn't supposed to be assembled. It had to be made and assembled simultaneously. I could cut, stamp, and crimp the teeth onto the cloth tape in one action. We worked together on a few ideas, and jotted them down on paper. It was a real breakthrough. Garth left, and I continued to modify his die. This was exciting. I had a new focus, and a purposeful use of my down time. With the proper design, we could produce a zipper at a much faster pace.

The days passed, and I healed well. I couldn't eat solid food, but I could mash my own vegetables, and cut my meat into bits. It had been two weeks and I was ready to get back to work.

Robert came by on a Sunday with a gift. He had a beer in his hand and some rolled up fabric. He handed it to me, 'I had Audrey and the girls make this up for you,' he said with a grin.

I unfurled it. A coat... with a hood. Almost identical to my coat, but made from two layers of unbleached linen, with leather strips on the shoulders to buffer the rain. It had buttons with a flap to conceal them. He held it up for me, so I could put it on. My shoulder was still tender.

'I love it!' I blurted. 'It's like my old coat.'

'Yes, it is. I drew up a pattern for the girls and it was all sewn on your machine...except for the leather and the buttons. They're done by hand.'

'What an incredible gift! I can't believe it.'

'Well, It's actually a toile. We're going to start making them. I thought, with modern machines, we required a modern product. Your stylish yellow and black coat was the inspiration.' We talked a while, and looked over my drawings as he finished his beer. I felt ready. It was time for me to return to work.

Chapter 8

Making up for Lost Time

I was sore and damaged, but invigorated. I lit a candle and laid out my clothes. It was a cool December morning. My new coat couldn't have come at a better time. There would be no way I could pull my jumper over my head. My collar bone and ribs were still too tender. Jacob brought in some tea and oats. Colleen knew I was going to work today, so I guess she sent him early. He was quiet and half asleep. I wanted to hit the ground running. My first order of business was to teach the girls a few tricks, and how to adjust the stitch on the machine.

Robert called the girls around to watch. We had six machines and a seventh near completion. The majority of the seamstresses continued sewing by hand, while I taught six at a time on the machines. All the girls had mastered a straight stitch, but didn't know anything about the functions or settings. So much of the complex stitching was still done by hand. I spent the entire morning teaching them each function; how to make button holes; how to adjust the length of a stitch; how to adjust the tension. Afterwards, they all practiced, six at a time. I wish we had a machine for each girl, they wanted to work on them all day. It was a motivational tool, they enjoyed using. There were 15 girls who lived in the back of the factory. They asked if they could practice at night. It brought back childhood memories when I learned to sew. I just wanted to make new things and the machine allowed me to do it quickly.

I suggested to Robert we let the girls practice at night. He immediately said no. I pulled him aside. 'Why can't the girls work after hours?'

'Because they're workers, not friends. If you allow them freedom, you'll lose command over them.'

That caught me off guard. I forgot it was a sweat shop in 45. It was a terrible way to rule a workforce. I thought, maybe I could advocate for them a little. 'I read an article about a factory in France that gave their employees some freedom, and they developed a loyalty to their employer. We could give each of them enough fabric to make a dress. It would be a small expense on our end, and the morale of our workers would be boosted.'

'I can't see it working out that way, besides, John would never agree to give them yards of linen for free.'

'What if you deducted from my wages,' I persisted.

'I don't know why you're so passionate about this.'

'It could be a Christmas bonus, better than being a Scrooge.'

'What's a Scrooge?' he asked.

'Scrooge. Charles Dickens. A Christmas Carol.'

'I've read his books. That must be a new one?'

I can only hope that book has already been published, 'Yes, it is. The moral of the story is his generosity paid off in productivity.'

'If you can convince John, I'll go along with your scheme.'

I went next door to discuss it with John. He didn't care much for the idea either. He said Robert ran the linen shop, and if he was OK with it, and I was covering the cost of the materials, then he was fine with it. I informed Robert and we discussed the particulars.

There were two doors to the workers quarters. The one leading to the factory was locked at night, the other exited outside. This was an issue; an outsider could enter the girl's quarters and walk right into the factory. We discussed rules for this arrangement.

Robert turned to me and said, 'Give them the good news.'

'Maybe you should tell them.'

Robert smiled and we both addressed the girls. He lit up, 'Ryan and I have discussed a provision for you. Something that will enable everyone additional time to practice on the sewing machines, when we shut down for the evening. I'll leave the factory door unbolted, and you'll each be provided enough linen to make yourselves a dress.'

All the girls clapped and screeched with excitement.

'Let me finish,' he said. 'You will not be able to bring anybody into the factory except your co-workers who don't live on the premises. This will be done on your own time, from now until we break for Christmas holidays.'

Robert turned, looked at me and smiled. I think he felt pretty good about it.

As Christmas approached, I kept my days light, but productive. I was able to use a foot operated loom in the mill, to create the tape for the zippers. It was basically a webbing, woven into long strips. The loom didn't require any modifications, the threads were simply set up in clusters. Several lengths of tape could be spun simultaneously. John designated one of his workers to produce thousands of yards of tape, in preparation for the zipper die. Matt created a button hole attachment to make sewing button holes easier. They were small metal pieces that sat under the needle foot, and guided the stitch. Another one of my stolen inventions. I spent a few hours a day with Garth modifying the zipper die. He welcomed the business, and hired additional men to assist with his added work load.

The girls learned quickly. They were using the machines to their fullest. We now had eight sewing machines, and were improving our methods of production. Every machine we added, produced as much merchandise as five hand sewers. We manufactured a glut of coats to sell, just before Christmas. Our retailers couldn't keep them stocked. It was the first time in history people could buy mass produced clothing off the rack, rather than having them tailor made. The convenience was making us the Amazon of our time, in fashion. The outlook for the year seemed limitless, but I knew it would be short lived. My knowledge of the future burdened me with guilt. Robert wanted to invest all his profits into expanding the building, to accommodate more sewing machines. I tried convincing him we should construct the 35 machines we needed for Feeney's Linens, and sell the rest to the tailors and factories around the country. The guaranteed money would be in selling sewing machines, since the linen industry in Ireland would die out, as the famine progressed. Any expansion should be in Dublin or Belfast. The blight had little effect on them, except for the migration of people leaving through their ports. Holding back my knowledge of the future weighed on my conscience, as our friendship strengthened.

The days before Christmas were counting down. The factory would close Christmas day and stay shut until January 5th. This was partially to allow people ample time to travel to visit family, but it was mostly economical. The retailers wouldn't purchase any new product until after their year-end inventory. This year was exceptional, because we caught up on all our back orders and we were filling new orders in record time. After a long satisfying week, I went back to Murphy's.

'Hello Mr. Ryan,' Stephen said, with a smile on his face. 'That case of whiskey you ordered came in today. I put it in your room.'

Thomond Gate Distillery. What a luxury. 'Thanks for ordering that for me. It's great whiskey.'

'I ordered a case for myself,' he said.

'I guess I'll have one of those, and a Guinness to wash it down please.'

He poured me a glass, and I sipped it. It was everything I remembered. It also got me through the initial shock of being anchored here. I finished it, and my Guinness, and had another.

Stephen and I talked in between serving customers.

'Are you ready for Christmas, Mr. Ryan?'

'I'm getting there. The whiskey covers a few gifts. What do you do for Christmas?'

'I close the pub for a few days, then we go to the farm, prepare a goose dinner and open our gifts.'

'That sounds nice,' I said.

'What about you Mr. Ryan? Are you doing anything special for Christmas? Any family?'

If only he knew. I wish I could see my family. Lying about my life was a skill I had become good at. It was my worst character trait, and it pained me that I could not be truthful to my friends.

'I can't visit family this year. I don't have any transportation.'

He twisted his head, 'All you need is a horse? You're from Kerry, aren't cha? That's a day's ride from here.'

I nodded. My ancestors were from Magherafelt. I had no family in Kerry, in 1845.

'I have a horse at the farm you can use.'

'I wouldn't want to...'

'It's no bother,' he said. 'The factory is shut down until January. What's stopping you?'

I was running out of excuses. I didn't have family anymore. In 1845 my family was still living in Magherafelt. 'My family is from Northern Ireland. We moved to Kerry from there.'

He seemed concerned about me being alone for Christmas, but this was my life now, in 45.

'How far north? Mayo, Donegal?' he asked.

That took me aback. Northern Ireland in this time is a direction, not a separate country. 'Magherafelt,' I replied.

'Here's what you do,' he insisted. 'You take the horse to Dublin.

It's a hard ride, but you can do it in a day. You go to the train station and pay to put the horse in the cattle car. You stay with the horse and you don't need to buy a ticket for yourself. It's only a few hours by train to Belfast. Your horse is all rested. Then you ride a few more hours and you're there.'

Wow. He makes it sound so easy, a four-hour drive by car.

Then it hit me, I did my ancestry search a few years ago. One of the documents I printed from the records was my great, great, great grandparent's marriage certificate. My grandfather was a saddler and he lived on Meeting Street. I don't know why I remembered that, but I knew where I could find him. I'm not sure if it was Stephen's persistence, or the alcohol, or the need for family, but I was bursting with passion.

'OK! I'll take the horse!'

Stephen smiled, he seemed quite proud of himself. Giving me family for Christmas. I was tripping. This was out there, but exciting.

'When are you leaving?' he asked.

'Early Christmas morning at 5.'

'I'll make sure young Stephen has it all ready for ya. Who are ya visiting?'

'My great.... My grandfather, he's a great guy.'

We sat and talked until my glass was empty. I retired to my room. When I opened the door, my case of whiskey was sitting there. If I could take that back to 21 it would be worth a year's pay, I thought. Maybe, this is why fate took my time machine away. I'd be going back and forth in time, just for whiskey. I couldn't wrap my head around the idea of meeting my great, great, great grandparents. I could picture the strip of paper from the ancestry records. His name was Samuel. Must have been popular in this time. Her name was Elizabeth, I think. Occupation-saddler. Magherafelt. Meeting Street. Now I needed to recall their children's names. I had a few days to prepare.

I pulled a bottle of whiskey from the crate, and knocked on Scotty's door. As the door opened my eyes watered from the stink. I handed him the bottle, and wished him a Happy Christmas. I dashed back to my room, inhaled my sweet air, and readied for my trip.

Monday morning, I entered the shop. Most of the girls were outfitted in white linen dresses. They must have worked all night throughout the week and all weekend. It was quite a spectacle, and gave the place an air of grace. Robert noticed it immediately and was proud to see his product on display. The girls were voguing our products for retail buyers who visited the factory. It almost looked formal. We stood at the back and looked over the workers.

'How cool is that?' I said proudly.

Robert looked at me strangely, 'I find it warm?'

I realized my slip, 'I mean how amazing is that? Cool, is kind of a Kerry slang. It's rhetorical.'

He looked at the girls, they appeared so uniform, 'Looks proper. Cool.'

'They're stitching faster, and they've learned some new tricks,' I added.

'I've noticed it too. Perhaps this scheme of yours isn't such a bad thing. It's good Christmas cheer, I must say.'

We both smiled and I admired my advocacy. The workers seemed extremely happy, and it made the sweat shop appear less oppressive. The girls caught up on everything so they were only producing the hooded coats. We were all happy about it. When my day ended, I headed straight to the general store, picked up a compass and some dried fruit for my trip.

The following day, was relaxed. I was in and out of the factory giving whiskey to Garth and his sons, Matt and his 2 apprentices. I picked out a large linen shirt for Stephen and a dress for Colleen from the warehouse. One of the girls wrapped them in pattern paper and string, then I added them to my tab. By Wednesday, we shipped out the last of the coats to the retailers and finished up for the year. I gave John a bottle of whiskey and took Robert's to the office. He pulled out 2 cups, uncorked his whiskey, and poured us a couple of shots.

'Happy Christmas,' he said as we toasted. 'I couldn't be happier with the progress, and what we've accomplished in a couple of months, gives me hope for the upcoming year.'

'Wait until next year,' I said. 'We'll create an assembly line.' Robert smiled. I'm not sure he realized how much time this would save. It made Ramsom Olds and Henry Ford rich men.

He reached into his desk and handed me a small box. 'Happy Christmas. This is from John and I.'

It was a silver pocket watch. I had lost track of time when I gave up my phone. I'm not sure that he was aware of how symbolic his gift was to me. This primitive time piece was the technology of this time and I was pleased to have it. I thanked him, finished my drink, and went to the pub.

The bar was half full of people and the Christmas cheer was evident. I ordered a beer and some food. Riding to Magherafelt was going to be a challenge. I spent many an afternoon taking a leisurely ride on my horse in 21, but this was going to be a hard enduring push. Colleen brought me my meal and told me to come by the kitchen in the morning, before I left. After eating, I wished Stephen a Happy Christmas, and retired to my room.

It was still dark when I awoke. I lit a candle and packed my saddle bags, checked my watch, and headed to the kitchen. There was a lamp burning and Colleen was prepping her Christmas goose. I handed her some gifts. Linen for her and Stephen and coins wrapped in tiny envelopes I had made from my paper, for the kids. Colleen examined the envelopes, weighing them in her palm, then handed them back.

'This is too much,' she said. 'These are pounds.'

'It's the least I can do. You and your family were there for me,'

'It's too much. I can't.'

'Look, It's for their future. For leaner times.'

'No!' she insisted. 'I can't take it.'

'You must. Experts have predicted another blight next year, and famine.'

'Experts? We've had blights and famine my entire life. I always prepare.'

'Yes, but next year will be tragic. They're recommending you don't plant potatoes next year. Anything but potatoes.'

'I've never heard of experts on this. Who told you this?'

'You're just going to have to believe me,' I insisted.

Colleen put the linen on the counter and tried handing back my wrapped coins.

I stepped back, 'I'll be insulted if you don't take my gifts.'

She took a breath and conceded, 'Thank you, Mr. Ryan. I've prepared you some food.'

She began stuffing a pillow case with a jar of beets, soda bread wrapped in a towel, a couple of beef sandwiches and a few apples.

She continued speaking as she loaded the food, 'You shouldn't be heading out, you've barely healed. You could be hurt or the horse.'

'Don't worry about the horse I...'

'I'm not worried about the horse. Your rent is paid until March it'll more than cover the horse,' she said with a stern tone. 'I was lucky to get it from you before those thugs robbed you.'

'I know,' I said. 'But...'

'Dublin has more people that will do you harm,' she said. 'And I don't want to see you getting into any more scraps. I don't know what Stephen told you about Dublin but it's a 2-day ride at best.'

She handed me the pillow case, wished me a Happy Christmas, gave me a hug. I went to the farm to get the horse. The young Stephen had it ready to go. It was too dark to ride, so I grabbed the reins and walked, contemplating the now 2-day journey to Dublin.

Chapter 9

Grandfather Time

Darkness forced me to guide my horse, before dawn lit my trail. When the sun rose, I rode hard for two hours, let my horse water and graze, and hit the trail hard again. Daylight dictated my pace. The winter sun was transient and the waning moon a sliver. Along the road the exodus had begun. Hundreds of people were migrating from rural areas to cities, in search of work, opportunity, or simply a meal. Rural people were distinctly different, they spoke little, or no English, had less means, and their diet was predominantly potatoes. The blight had driven many of them from livelihood, and landlords from their homes. The lucky few would be emigrating to an unstable future in a foreign country, on crowded coffin ships. I was witnessing a history I had known. A book I had read. Pictures I had seen in black and white moving around me in full colour, yet tinged with grey. It was a sad reality on a course I couldn't change. As I cantered through towns, the numbers grew. Homeless people moving east towards Dublin or south to Cork, seeking work or a ship out. I had reached the Fort of Maryborough. The half way point to Dublin. There was too much desperation around me to stop, so I trudged on.

At the edge of town was a grain mill. There would be no time for grazing and I needed fuel for the push to Dublin. I purchased a sack of feed for the horse, and continued east. The cold, wet, and dark, ascended in unison. I needed shelter. Down a path off the road, was a derelict castle. The wind was fierce and bitter. This castle would house us both. As I approached the doorway, I could see the glow of a fire and heard a man's voice. I stopped, then heard a child cry. We were desperate for shelter. I dismounted and entered, leading my horse.

'Hello!' I shouted.

The hammering wind dampened my cry. I moved down the dark hallway towards the lucent fire. A man charged at me with a stick. I cowered, raised my hand, and cried, 'Wait!'

I heard a woman's voice, 'Timothy don't.'

He stood above me with his club raised, 'What do you want?'

'I just want shelter,' I cried.

'Go somewhere else!'

'OK. I'm leaving.'

I turned and the woman cried out, 'Timothy don't do this. It's Christmas.'

'Wait,' he said reluctantly. 'Come in.'

'Thank you.' I stepped into the light, then reached out my hand and shook his, 'I'm Ryan.'

'I'm Timothy and this is Abigail,' he gestured to his wife glowing by the fire. 'My son William.'

William was a young boy around two. As my eyes adjusted, the room was revealed. It was a great chamber made of cut stone with two large pine trees growing against the walls acting as a roof. Timothy had a horse and cart beside one of the trees, blankets laid on the ground and a fire in the centre. Abigail and William were glowing by the fire. I pulled the sack of grain and began feeding my horse.

I looked at Timothy, 'Can I give some to your horse?'

He had a serious look on his face but nodded. I removed my saddle bags and saddle, unfurled my blanket on the opposite side of the fire, and pulled out my pillow case of food. Abigail glared as I began eating half of my sandwich. Picking up the napkin with the other half, I leaned across, 'Please. Have this.'

Timothy looked apprehensive, but she needed no coaxing. Reaching out with both hands, she grasped it, took a bite, and inhaled with pleasure. She held it for William, took another bite, and handed it to Timothy. He looked at me and nodded.

I reached in my saddlebag and pulled out a small box of dried fruit, took a few pieces and offered it to Abigail, 'Have some,' I said, then gestured to William and Timothy to take some too. They were a young family but looked worn from their hardship, 'Where are you from?'

Timothy answered with a full mouth, 'Westport, Mayo. We're going to Dublin, then America.'

'Are you a farmer?'

'I was,' he replied. 'We lost our crop.'

Abigail began crying. I pulled out some soda bread, broke off a piece and handed it to her, 'America will be good. You can make a good life there.'

She broke off pieces of bread for the family, then put the larger piece in a small cloth bag. We spoke for a while, and fell asleep on our blankets.

I woke up, lit a candle, and fed the horse a few handfuls of feed. Timothy woke. 'Thanks for the food,' he whispered.

I began saddling the horse, 'We need to look out for each other.' I slung the saddle bags onto my horse and pulled out the jar of beets Colleen had given me. 'Take these.'

He nodded no.

'It's OK. I don't like them,' I said in a soft voice.

He reached out and took them, and nodded.

I felt through my pockets and pulled out two shillings, 'Take this too,' I pleaded.

'I thank you for the food, sir,' he said quietly. 'But I don't need charity.'

He clearly did need assistance, and it was nothing for me to give. I noticed a brass tea kettle in his cart, shimmering in the candle light. 'Sell me the kettle?' I asked, as I pointed to his cart.

He took the two shillings and handed me the kettle and nodded. We whispered our goodbyes as I led my horse out and down the road.

The morning was cold and dark, so I walked briskly towing my horse. At the first glimmer of sunlight, I began riding, picked up to a trot, ran full tilt and back to a trot. The people kept moving. Hundreds of blight refugees walking, riding, and towing carts, heading east to Dublin. All of them with the same affliction. I watched the flow of people as I rode down from the hilltop. It felt like a period movie shot from a drone. Unfortunately, I knew how it would end. I felt helpless. There was no, 'Go Fund Me.' No sympathetic ear. I trotted on. Finally entering Dublin.

Daylight was still with me. The historic buildings dominated the skyline. I could visualize the new buildings that replaced the ones, I saw now. Trinity college was timeless. It's as old now as it was in 21. It gave me some sense of connection. The years I'd spent there, were where my mechanical, manufacturing and computer skills were born. Those skills brought me here, in this time. An eerie thought, and a sad irony. There was noise and smoke. Wheels on stone. Horses and people moving about. Talking, yelling, laughing, and crying. The music of anguish. My senses were perked. I scanned the sky for signs of progress. There were no street lights.

No electric poles. No turbines spinning in the River Liffey. Electricity must have been a long way off. It gave me a sense of despair. This time and mine, had no overlap.

I came across a market and filled my pillowcase with apples, carrots, and fresh soda bread. They pointed me towards the station. I wove through a field of beggars with beckoning hands, until I reached the train station, and paid for my ticket. Waiting in the brush beside the tracks, I let my horse graze, then sat and contemplated my introduction to my 3rd great grandparents. Who was I going to be? What was my lineage? Would they catch me in a lie? With limited knowledge of my distant relatives, I worried they'd be skeptical. The reality was I was a stranger showing up at their door.

The smoke appeared long before the roar of the train. My horse followed as I led him to the back of the platform, and waited in a fenced in section with another man and his cows. We were greeted by an agent and boarded. The train car floor was covered in straw. There was a water trough in the middle with a metal bucket beside it. I untied the feed sack from the pommel and fed the horse, then dipped the bucket in the trough and put it down for him to drink. The farmer tended his cows.

Forty-five minutes had passed, and we arrived at the Drogheda Station. This was my stop. The only stop. Not 3 hours, and not near Belfast as Stephen had professed. It still saved me hours of riding, and gave me a chance to refuel and rest my horse.

The sun was setting as we left the station, and I rode until dark. Passing through the town of Dundalk, I came upon a bridge. My shelter for the evening. We bedded down for the night. Romanticising about uniting with my family kept me motivated but restless.

It was 4 in the morning and I couldn't sleep. I was too agitated and guided the horse to a dark field to refuel, occasionally giving him handfuls of grain. Pacing, I contemplated meeting my distant ancestors. There was no instruction booklet for this. Every introduction, required me to perjure my true self. My secret past was the future. The deception was necessary, but the guilt was inevitable and weighed on me.

With the horse fed, we walked the road north. Crowds of people were heading towards Belfast. A sad site to see. The sun rose in Newry and I saw a woman lying at the side of the road. People just walked past. As I inched closer, I could see she had perished and her feet were bare. They were clean and unblemished. The needy harvesting from the dead. Angry and saddened, I rode on. An hour down the road, another body, but I knew not to stop. There was a constant feeling of resentment. This was not my time, or my tragedy. It didn't belong to me. It felt for a moment, these people weren't my people, and I was only an observer. My bout of self-pity would be followed by reflection. How selfish was I to think that anyone deserved this blight?

Anger drove me forward, pushing the horse hard to Magherafelt. Shops were closed, but the city was prosperous. There was little sign of despair. I poked my head in several stores to ask directions, leading me to Meeting Street. It seemed metaphorical. There was a butcher shop at the corner. He looked familiar with his apron covered in blood. Dexter, from the TV show. He looked just like him. I tried not to smirk.

'I'm looking for Samuel McCullough, the saddler. He lives on this block.'

'Yes,' he replied. 'He's just down the road, past the brown house. Just keep walking straight until you see the bakery with a green awning. Then, you'll see four, two story homes attached. He's in the last one, by the alley, his shop is in the back.'

'Thank you.' I said. 'How far down is it?

'It's only half way down the street.'

I peered at his display, 'I guess I'll take the corned beef.'

He wrapped it in waxed paper, wrapped it again and tied it with cord. I paid and left, walking my horse slowly down the road. I rushed for days to reach this moment. My body felt tense as I contemplated what to say. The whole thing was just absurd. I knocked on the door.

A young woman in her 20's opened it and screamed, 'Joseph!'

There were footsteps running up the alley beside the house. A young man appeared with a mallet and a pick in his hands. He looked at me with frightened eyes, then whimpered, 'Da. You look like my Da.'

I couldn't believe the resemblance. He was a man in thirties and looked like me when I was 20 years younger. We both stood there speechless. The family resemblance was undeniable.

'I'm looking for Samuel. I'm his cousin.'

'I'm Samuel,' he replied.

I was expecting an old man and never considered that he'd be young. I turned to the woman, 'You're Elizabeth?'

'Eliza,' she replied.

I fought to find the right words, 'I'm Ryan. McCullough. You're 3rd cousin.'

'You look just like Joseph,' she replied.

'Joseph?'

'My Da,' replied Samuel.

There was no preparing for the thoughts and feelings running through my head. Staring at my distant relatives gave me a feeling of happiness and awe that words could not describe.

'You're like my father raised from the grave,' he said. He patted my shoulder. 'Let's put your horse in the back.'

He had a workshop with a small stable, backing onto a field, separated by a fence, with a gate. 'Where are you riding from?' he asked.

'Doonass, County Claire.'

'Oh Lord, that's a long way. Where are you staying?'

'Nowhere yet.'

'You'll stay here. I'll put a cot in Joseph's room.'

I didn't argue. There was nowhere else I wanted to be, but here. He started untying the feed sack from the pommel and handed it to me. Then pulled off the saddle bags and straddled them on my shoulder. He removed the saddle, opened the gate, and let the horse out in the field. He wiped his hands on his pants and said, 'Let's go inside.'

Eliza had bread and butter on the table.

'So how was your Christmas?' she asked.

I had forgotten about Christmas. I didn't think to bring a gift. 'I was travelling here,' I replied. 'So, my Christmas was on the road.'

I sat at the table and set my saddle bags down. The kettle clanged as it hit the floor. 'I brought you this,' I said, as I untied it from the saddle bags. 'It's not new but it's brass.'

She picked it up, cupped the corner of her apron with her palm, gave it a quick polish. 'That's too expensive a gift to give. We're practically strangers, but I love it. You're too kind.'

I reached down into my saddle bags, 'There's more.' I pulled out the pillow case of food, the corned beef and 2 bottles of whiskey, setting them on the table.

Samuel looked at me with a serious stare, 'You can't be a relative

67

of mine.' My heart stopped. 'No relative of mine would bring us meat or whiskey or fine gifts.' He laughed. We all did. Living in history as a time traveller was something I never took lightly. It was a privilege; no amount of money could buy. Seeing my ancestors and spending time with them was the ultimate gift.

He turned to Eliza, 'Ryan's going to stay with us.'

'Well then. I'll put down the cot in Joseph's room,' she went upstairs.

'So how are we related?' asked Samuel.

My eyes were focused on him. It was like looking at myself in the past. The resemblance quelled my fear of being rejected. These people weren't jaded like my generation. 'I'm a cousin. Third, I think. Or removed. I don't really understand how second, third or once removed all fits together, but there's no doubt we're related.'

'There's no denying that,' he said, as he looked me up and down.

His house was sparse, simple, and clean. There was no decorations or Christmas tree. I wasn't sure if the tradition came later or his struggle was hard.

He looked at me, then at the whiskey, 'Might we break the seal?'

'Absolutely.'

I pulled the cork, he grabbed 2 glasses, and I poured us a drink. He took a sip. Picked up the bottle, and peered at the label, 'Aged 7 years. The good stuff.'

I knew the blight would be tough on him. Without farmers he would lose a portion of his market.

'I was thinking of buying a saddle,' I said. 'Do you have one?'

'I started one for a friend but he lost his crops and left. It's for a smaller horse. It won't fit yours.'

'That's not my horse,' I replied with a smile.

'It'll take me a few days to finish. How long are you here for?'

'A couple of days at least. What if I help you?'

'Have you ever saddled?'

'I'm a tailor by trade.'

'That'll do. Come. I'll show ya.' He went to the stairs, yelled to Eliza, 'We're going out back.'

'Wait!' she cried. 'I'm bringing down young Joseph.'

She came down with Joseph, he was about 18 months old. I remember my great, great grandfather was George, so this must be his older brother.

We headed out back with our glasses as Samuel grabbed the

whiskey from the table. He flaunted his work bench with pride and caressed the saddle. It was stretched over a barrel shaped stand made of wood, about a meter off the ground.

'This is it,' he boasted. 'It needs stirrups. I have to set the cantle, the billet and add some detailing.'

'Let's get at er,' I said.

Samuel smiled and we got to work. I could see the pride he took in his craft. An hour on, Eliza walked in carrying two corned beef sandwiches with cabbage. 'Better get some food in ya, or you'll both be drunk by dark.' She pulled a glass from her apron pocket, filled it with whiskey, and took it to the house.

We sat on stools and ate our sandwiches. Samuel pointed to my boots. 'Where did you get those?'

'They were shipped from China.'

'They look exotic,' he said. 'All the way from China.' He reached down and touched them. Then stood beside me and matched his boot to mine. 'We're the same size,' he said. 'Can I try them on?'

I pulled them off and stood there in my socks. He pulled off his boots and tried mine on. He had tan leather boots with incredible workmanship. Barely worn. I picked up one of his boots, 'These are nice. Where did you get them?'

'I made em.'

'You made them?'

'I make saddles. I can make boots.'

I slipped his boots on and walked in a circle. 'Wow these are really nice.'

'You like em do ya?'

I smiled, 'They're great!'

'You wanna trade?'

'Trade? It wouldn't be fair.'

'I'll give you a family discount on the saddle.'

'I meant it wouldn't be fair to you Samuel. I love them!'

'And I think these are grand. What do you call this?' he asked as he rubbed his thumb and fore finger in the cuff.

'Vulcanized rubber.'

'You could make saddles from this. So, we have a deal?'

'Definitely,' I replied.

My head filled with metaphors. I felt privileged to literally walk in his shoes, work with him in his shop, and share food and whiskey. Of all my experiences, good and bad, this moment made being trapped in time worth it.

He had a real talent for his craft. He marked the leather and had me punch holes for the stitching, correcting my technique from time to time, then focused on the finishing work. We worked and laughed until the sun set and went inside.

Eliza had Joseph in a high chair, while she was making dinner. She looked at us as we came in the door, and pointed to our boots, 'Take your boots off.' She walked up to Samuel, took the half bottle of whiskey from his hand, and put it in the cupboard. She laughed, 'I think you've both had enough to drink.' Then pointed at our boots as we removed them. 'How did that come about?'

'We traded,' Samuel said.

'No,' she said. 'Take your boots back Ryan, he's taking advantage of you. He made those from left over leather.' She walked over and picked up a rubber boot and examined it, 'These are from China. I'm sure they're expensive,' she said as she inspected the sole. 'They have so much detail. You'll be feeling swindled in the morning when you're sober.'

'I'm happy with the deal,' I said. 'They're one of a kind.'

She poured us some water and had us sit down, then made corned beef and cabbage with carrots. It wasn't for lack of imagination; it was for lack of refrigeration. You eat it before it spoils. We all laughed and finished our meal, then talked for hours about work, family, and the blight. I gave them the same story about experts predicting another blight next year, to prepare them for the worst and told them what I had seen on the road. Eliza put Joseph to bed and I followed shortly after. As I laid awake, I relived my day, then fell asleep.

I heard Samuel in the kitchen and went downstairs. It was after 5 in the morning and he had the new kettle on the stove.

'Tea?' he asked in a subdued voice.

'Yes. Please.'

Eliza came down with Joseph, breast fed him in the other room and set him on a blanket on the floor, 'How you fairing today?'

'Fine,' we replied simultaneously.

'Let me make you some eggs.'

She pulled the kettle from the stove and we sat down. We drank tea, then a second cup. We ate our eggs and carried our tea to the back door. As I put on my new leather boots, Samuel smiled. The deal was set.

The shop smelled of leather, lanolin, and beeswax. A smell that filled me with comfort. I consumed every moment. Samuel lit the lantern, then began organizing his tools. I began sweeping. He explained what we needed to accomplish for the day and set me up with some tasks. He shared stories about his father and mother. How his mother died giving birth to his youngest brother. He told me how his father, who was also a saddler had lived with them until he died a year ago. We worked all morning and almost finished the saddle. Eliza came in with lunch. The last of the corned beef, some carrots and cabbage. A while later she came back, took our plates, and returned with the half bottle of whiskey and three glasses.

'Joseph is down for a nap,' she said as she handed us a glass of whiskey. 'It turned out nice.' She pulled up a stool and watched as we finished up on the saddle. I straddled it while Samuel set the cantle. Eliza topped up her whiskey and headed back to the house.

Samuel was notching some details in the leather, 'Would you like your initials carved in?'

'You should carve in yours. It's a work of art and you're the artist.'

He smiled and carved them in, then mixed up some lanolin, beeswax and stain and handed me a rag. We drank, polished the saddle, and laughed. The sun began setting and I knew I'd be leaving in the morning. He took my money for the saddle and I offered to pay him more but he refused. I had no idea what the material cost was but he could scarcely have made a profit. I offered to pay more but he rejected me again. We went back into the house, took off our boots and Eliza told us to sit down.

The room was filled with the smell of fresh baked bread and cabbage. She poured us some water, put some butter, sliced bread, and cabbage soup on the table. The smells filled my heart and soul. It gave me comfort. I would carry these brief memories with me for a lifetime. The meal was simple and wholesome and the conversation was too. They were decent people and I was proud to be related to them. We exchanged addresses, promised to write, and told them I'd be leaving early in the morning, then went to bed. There was a real connection that only family could have. The smell of the house reminded me of my granny's home. I relished the day, then fell asleep.

Five o'clock came quickly. Samuel and Eliza were in the kitchen talking. I got up and took 3 gold coins and hid them under the cot. I knew this would help them in leaner times and in a strange way, may have been insuring my own prosperity. I laughed at the thought of how this might impact the future, then went downstairs.

'Have some tea,' she said as she pulled out a chair.

I sat down, drank some tea. The three of us talked while Eliza made us breakfast. We ate and I got up to leave.

'Wait,' Eliza said. She began wrapping some buttered bread in the clean piece of butcher paper she had salvaged from the beef and tied it with the butcher's cord, then put it in my pillow case with some apples. She gave me a firm hug, 'Thank you for everything. It's been a pleasure. Don't forget to write and let us know that you got back safely.'

I put on my new boots, went out with Samuel, got my horse, and strapped on the saddle. Samuel buckled my new saddle around its neck, then tethered it to the pommel with strips of leather.

I turned to him, 'Thanks for everything. It was great to meet you.'

'Thank you,' he said. 'You made our Christmas. It's been a tough go for the last few months, your gifts and the money for the saddle really made a difference. Your generosity really uplifted us both.' He looked down at his rubber boots, 'And these are just grand.'

He put out his hand to shake and I gave him a hug. He patted me on the back and I led my horse down the dark alley out to the road.

'Be safe out there,' he said.

I turned down Meeting Street and felt a sense of family, with Samuel's boots and Eliza's bread.

Chapter 10

From Linen Rags to Riches

The long ride home gave me time to reflect on my good fortune. Finding family and landing a good job likely saved my life. Passing the downhearted faces along the road gave me perspective. Maybe I have a purpose, to change a life or many. The outlook for my new year will contrast with millions of my brothers and sisters. I navigated through Dublin's dockyards, weaving through crowds of people. They were on their last hope with only one option. To leave everything and everyone they knew, never to see them again. An experience I could relate to. The solace I had carried from Meeting Street had eroded. The people on the road were now facing me as I passed. History had already written their fate, and it read in their empty eyes. As I neared home, the crowds diminished. My humble quarters welcomed me.

In the morning Jacob arrived with tea and oatmeal and restocked my wood and turf. I brought the empty dishes to the sink in the yard. Hearing Colleen in the kitchen, I wandered in, 'Good morning.'

'Good morning, Mr. Ryan, did you have a Happy Christmas?'

'Yes. Wonderful, and you?'

'Grand, just grand. Did you enjoy the beets?'

'Oh yes they were delicious, my granny wants your recipe.'

She blushed, 'I made them with vinegar like any other recipe, but I add cloves.'

'I'll tell her when I write.'

'Where's the jar?' she asked.

'We ate them.'

'What did you do with the jar?'

Strangely that sounded like something my granny in 21 would have asked. 'Oh yes, I… I broke it,' I replied, then changed the subject. 'Well thanks for the horse. It really made my Christmas.'

'Well, I'm glad. Family makes all the difference in these times. The children were overjoyed with your gift. I put it away for them, for when they're older. Except for young Stephen. He's old enough to budget.'

'Yes. He thanked me when I returned the horse. If you haven't any new tenants lined up, I'd like to stay. I'll pay you for the entire year in advance.'

'A year?' she asked. 'Well of course.'

It worked out to less than a week's pay for me. I could secure a place to live and help them out at the same time. Eventually, I would buy a farm, something few Irishmen could do in this time. This place was convenient and the Murphys were good people to be around. I would have never survived Samuel's attack had Stephen not stepped in, or the rest of the family hadn't nursed me back to health.

'I'll get that rent to you tomorrow.'

'Well thank you Mr. Ryan. You know where to find me.'

I went to my room and wrote my young granny a letter, informing her I had returned safely. I'm sure it would reach her in month. I relaxed my saddle-sore ass and fell asleep before sunset.

My new working year had arrived. I was rested, healed and enthusiastic.

Robert was energized, 'Good morning, Ryan. Did you have a Happy Christmas?'

'I sure did. I got to visit my grandparents and relax for a few days. How was yours?'

'Wonderful. I found the book you spoke of. "A Christmas Carol," by Charles Dickens.'

'Did you like it?'

'Riveting. My wife and I read it to the children. We couldn't stop. We finished it in a couple of days. I've always liked his writing and this one really stretched the imagination.'

Little did he know the hardship that book brought Dickens. His publishers swindled him by printing illicit copies. He eventually bankrupted his publisher, racked up legal fees, and lost his royalties.

We gazed over the factory. The women seemed exceptionally happy. The entire staff was dressed in white linen. Robert smiled as he saw the appeal of a uniformed staff, 'I think this may become a tradition. We should allocate materials every year for new dresses. It's impressive to the clients that visit our establishment.'

'Yes, it certainly sets us apart from other manufacturers and shows social character. We are in the garment business. If the women are dressed in rags, it looks bad on us.' I added.

Robert was ecstatic with the outcome, 'I'm going to have Audrey and 8 of the girls continue working on the new coats. The buyers have already sold out the ones we made before Christmas. I wish we had more machines. I have dozens of orders. The appeal of buying clothing without waiting for it to be made, is an option retailers are excited about.'

'Off the rack,' I said.

'I like the way that sounds. Coats sold off the rack. I'm going to use that to promote them,' Robert said with a smile.

This would be the first time in history clothing was made to sell off the rack at a large scale. There were certain hand sewn items available to buy, but generally clothing was custom made either by the woman of the house or a tailor. Hassle free shopping would unleash a rush of business and we had already seen the results from our Christmas sales.

'Perhaps we should make them in a few sizes, then people would be able to choose a size as if it were custom made.' I suggested.

'That's a great idea.'

'I saw Garth before I left for holidays. He said, he would have enough parts completed to build 5 or 6 machines by the time I got back. He only closed for two days over Christmas. We could have them built in a few days. It's not taking us as long to assemble them as it used to.'

Robert was bursting with enthusiasm. 'I have good news,' he said with a smile. 'We've purchased a building in town. We're converting it into a foundry and sewing machine factory.'

'That's great!'

'Yes. We've hired Garth's son Brett, to oversee the construction of the foundry, and we have a large crew of men working on it as we speak. Brett will be running it when it's finished.'

'How does Garth feel about it?'

'We've assured him we will continue to use his services at the capacity we did in the past. We need him to make all our brass components for the machines, as well as our zippers and any overflow. He'll have more work than ever. He seems happy with the arrangement.'

'This is incredible,' I said. 'We need to diversify. They predict this blight may last years. It may force our flax farmers to switch to a sustenance crop or leave.'

'We can do both,' he replied. 'We've had blights before. They've never affected our crops. We'll sell linen products, and sewing machines. I've already taken orders for a couple of sewing machines from two local tailors, and we've begun soliciting orders from abroad. We will be very wealthy men before years end, my friend.'

Having a market from abroad was key to surviving the famine years. He had no idea how this would benefit his future when the linen industry collapsed. In this time, it employed at least a million people in Ireland. It was dependent on a large labour force. First the farmers grew the flax, followed by retting and breaking the fibres. The fibres are then scrutched, heckled, spun, woven, and bleached. It involved an incredible amount of manual labour. In my time it was reduced to a handful of mills and a few tourist attractions. History has proven the success of the sewing machine. The real money will be when the rest of the world copies and builds our machine, and pays us royalties. Like they did with Mr. Singer.

A wagon with two men arrived from the blacksmith's shop. They had parts for several sewing machines, and our zipper die. It was only the size of a kitchen stove but weighed at least 200 kilos. It had three pistons that were driven by centrifugal force. One piston cut the brass and one shaped it into a zipper tooth. The third folded and crimped it onto the cloth tape, in rapid unison. We unloaded it at the mill. John, Robert, and I, hooked the die up to a belt and attached it to the mill wheel, driven by the flow of the River Shannon. We spent the next three days tweaking and adjusting it while Matt's team assembled the sewing machines. I loaded the brass ribbon and the cloth tape into the feed, then engaged the clutch. It began stamping out teeth. We sped it up gradually, until it reached full capacity. We were able to make 8 meters of zippers a minute. John was thrilled. He trained one of his workers to run the machine, and another to assemble the tabs, stoppers, and other parts onto the zippers.

The zipper not only had a modern and exciting appeal, it allowed us to produce our coats hours faster than a button up. This too would have a market for other clothing manufacturers. Everything was going well, until our lawyer gave us the bad news. Our sewing machine and zipper patents were being contested by an American named, Elias Howe. He claimed we had stolen his lockstitch sewing machine design, and his automatic continuous clothing closure. The zipper. Who knew the inventor of the sewing machine and zipper, were the same person? I knew they were stolen ideas, and this scenario could possibly arise. He accused us of espionage, spying and intellectual theft. He was furious. What he couldn't do was fight it. Apparently, he was still in the final throws of producing his sewing machine. It was almost identical to ours, except it was hand cranked without a treadle and extremely slow. He had not yet filed for a patent, so he had no legal grounds to pursue. He hadn't contested the patent we filed on the zipper die, just the zipper. The zipper die was the key to producing the zipper quickly. Like me, he initially hadn't designed a process of manufacturing the zipper that would enable him to produce them rapidly. He hadn't applied for a patent on the zipper either and was still in the testing stage of it. We had only beaten him by a few months on both patents. I wasn't sure that we were the ones that had taken his design away from him. In my time, Singer was the inventor of the sewing machine, I never even heard of Elias Howe. In any case, we beat them both.

It's times like this I wish I could Google the history of the sewing machine. I would be able to see when he filed for a patent, and find out how Mr. Singer fit into all this.

The winter months were productive. We had 40 machines in Feeney's Linens and additional workers for cutting and pinning. We had sold several sewing machines locally and a few to England. Word was spreading and I knew from history that it would. Our jackets were selling off the rack faster than we could make them. We had sold thousands of metres of zippers to garment manufactures throughout Ireland, England, and France. Garth built us a second zipper die to keep up with demand. Our zipper sales financed the construction of the sewing machine factory. The famine had provided us with a limitless work force and we were able to complete the factory by mid-March. John, Robert, and I went to Murphy's to celebrate.

Mary came to our table, 'Hello Mr. Ryan.' she said with a smile. 'Would you gentleman like some drinks?'

John shouted, 'Three whiskeys please!'

'And two Guinness,' Robert followed.

Mary returned with our drinks.

John picked up his glass and turned to me, 'A toast to Ryan, who has brought us good fortune and has taken us into a modern age.'

We toasted and drank back our whiskey in one gulp.

John ordered three more. 'Well Ryan,' he said. 'I knew there was something special about you when I saw that yellow coat. You've brought us great wealth and much more to come.'

'You've done me a service by taking me on. I couldn't be happier with the outcome.'

We were all very happy. Mary returned with our whiskey.

'What's on the menu for today,' Robert asked.

'Hamburgers,' she replied.

'Hamburger? What's that?'

'It's minced beef…'

He interrupted, 'I thought you said ham?'

She looked at me and said, 'You'll have to talk to Mr. Ryan about that. It's one of his creations.'

John laughed, 'Your inventive spirit has no bounds. We'll have three of those please.'

We continued speaking about the prospects for the sewing machines world-wide. John was gearing up to hire a team of sales men to sell them, and suggested Robert and I teach the buyers how they are used. I continued to discuss the concept of an assembly line that would speed up production. The energy was flowing and so were the drinks.

Mary returned with our meals, 'This is a hamburger. This is the roll, and the beef, onion, pickle, mustard, and..' she looked up at me for an answer.

'Mayonnaise and a side of coleslaw.' If only we had chips, I thought.

We all dug in. They were great. Colleen had baked fresh rolls. It was a fantastic burger. John and Robert loved them. We had more drinks. John was doubling up on the whiskey and got drunk, then left in a coach. Robert and I stayed and talked. We had been friends for a long time. I had held my secret from the moment I landed here. We were both drunk and I had been dying to tell someone from the beginning. I had to stop myself.

Robert interrupted my thoughts, 'You really have taken us in a novel direction. You've brought us into the future.'

Then it came blurting out of my mouth, and I couldn't stop it, 'I am from the future. I invented a time machine.'

Chapter 11

Tell Time

I just told Robert I was from the future and he looked at me, like I told him it was Tuesday.

I peered into his eyes, 'I'm from the future and I built a time machine.'

'Yes, you are. I've always seen you as a renaissance man. Your abilities can't be matched and I wouldn't doubt for a minute that you could build a clock.'

'There's no clock,' I persisted. 'I came here from the future using a machine I built.'

Robert smiled, 'I didn't think you had that much whiskey.'

'Grab your beer. Come with me.'

We went back to my room. I lit a candle, pulled out some paper, and began sketching my time machine. Robert sat on the edge of my bed and watched.

'I came from the year 2021 with this machine,' I said, as I pointed with my pencil to my sketch.

Robert smiled, 'I've seen the article.'

'There is no article!' I cried. 'The machine is gone. That's why I'm trapped here.'

Robert just looked at me with a smile on his face.

'You don't believe me? I don't blame you. How could you? Why would anybody?' I got up from the table and rummaged through a whiskey crate in the corner of my room, then pulled out my wallet,' This is my wallet from 2021.' I handed the money to Robert, 'This is our money. Look at the colour, the dates, it's Euros. The currency of my time.'

The five-pound notes in this time were large and white, with black ink and a watermark. Robert examined the money, as he rubbed it through his fingers, then squinted at the type. I pulled out the credit cards. 'These are credit cards. We use them in lieu of cash. They're made of plastic. A material that won't be invented for another 70 or 80 years.'

Robert's smile dropped and his mouth hung open, 'How is this possible?' He drew his finger across the card and examined the hologram on the back, 'This can't be. It's inconceivable you could come from a future time and travel to this time. Your machine doesn't even have wheels.'

'We refer to it as time travel,' I said, as I handed him my driver's license.

He looked at me, then at my license, 'Do you require a license to drive this, time travel machine? Does everyone have one?' He held it up to the candle light, amazed at the clarity of the picture, the hologram, and the clear plastic coating.

'No. The license is for driving an automobile…and I'm the only person with a time machine…well, that I know of.'

'This is too fanciful to believe. How would it even work? What's an auto?'

'An automobile is a horseless carriage. It runs on petrol, the waste product derived from kerosene. Newer models run on electricity stored in a battery. My time machine used electricity. It was far more advanced than our automobiles.'

Robert was curious, fascinated and hugely skeptical, 'It's hard to believe. It's physically impossible,' he said.

'I know how it sounds. It would be hard for someone in my time to believe it too. You don't even have electricity yet.' Robert was hard to read. How could I really size up anyone's reaction after I told them I was from the future.

'What about the autocarriage?' he asked.

'It's an automobile. It's like a steam engine. You can drive it from here to Dublin in 2 hours'

Robert just looked at me. Glancing at the table with the money and cards. Occasionally picking up my license to re-examine it.

'You can fly on an airplane to Dublin in 30 minutes,' I insisted. I pushed on in hopes that I could convince him somehow, 'We landed on the moon in 1969.'

'You jest.'

'I kid you not. An American astronaut, Neil Armstrong, was the first man to walk on the moon. A rocket took a three-man crew there in 4 days.'

'Impossible.'

I picked up the newspaper beside the fireplace. There was an article about the repeal of the corn tariffs. Something we learned in school. Britain in this time had high grain tariffs on cheaper foreign grain to make locally grown grains competitive. They were expensive and benefited the rich land owners. All grains fell under the corn tariff laws. The prime minister had repealed the tariffs in hopes it would allow cheaper foreign grain into the country to help alleviate the famine. It divided the Conservative Party and eventually forced Sir Robert Peel to resign. I pointed to the article, 'You see this,' I said, as Robert eyed the article. 'This action will cause Sir Robert to resign before years end. This year's potato crop will be hit by a blight worse than last year's. 1847 is known as Black 47 in history books. We will suffer mass starvation and mass emigration. It continues until 1852. Many of the linen mills here will not survive it.'

Robert seemed to take me more seriously, 'What happens to our mill?'

'We didn't cover specific mills in history class. Just the linen industry in general. Many of them lose their workers to emigration or starvation.' It was hard to know what he was thinking, 'We're seeing lots of famine and despair already. You will see it escalate this year. Next year it will peak. By 1852 we will have a million deaths and a million more people emigrate from Ireland.'

Robert sat with a sad expression, 'I can only hope none of this is true.'

'When Sir Robert resigns this year, you'll know I'm not making this up. Elias Howe really was the inventor of the sewing machine. My design is copied from an old Singer sewing machine. For some reason in my time, a man by the name of Singer is known as the man that invented the sewing machine, not Elias Howe.'

Robert raised a brow, 'We received a letter from Isaac Singer's barrister. It had no legal merit so I didn't mention it.'

A huge weight had been lifted from my conscience. It felt cleansing. Telling the truth was an amazing feeling. To finally unburden myself of this secret was liberating. There was no stopping my words. I had to get them out. 'I had been working on these time machines in my spare time for years. In 2020 we had a pandemic. I lost my wife and my job. That entire year I worked on finishing my time machines. They were never designed to propel me through time. They were supposed to propel me hundreds of miles instantaneously.'

Robert just stared at me as I spoke, I knew he was skeptical.

'In April of 2021, I completed two machines. The larger one was a prototype that I attached to a sheep and sent her back in time. Then I put mine on and arrived here in October of 1845.'

Robert sat quietly for a moment, 'I thought this was a ruse at first, when you drew the sketch of your time machine. I thought you were merely copying the steam engine sheep from the article in the paper.'

'What article?'

'The article I was trying to tell you about. In the paper. They called it, "The Steam Engine Sheep," and it was wearing that device,' he said as he tapped his finger on my sketch. 'They had an illustration of a sheep in the paper, wearing your machine.'

I was stunned. My mind went blank, 'What did the article say?'

Robert searched his memory for an answer, 'Well, it mentioned that it was found by a farmer. They called it a steam engine sheep because of the apparatus that was tied to it…'

'Where was it found? Did they mention who the farmer was?'

'It was last year sometime, before I met you.'

'Was it in Clifden?'

'I don't remember exactly,' he said awkwardly.

I couldn't believe it. My time machine is here. Somewhere. I've got to find it, 'What paper was it in?' I asked as I paced the room.

'I'm not sure. It could have been the Examiner, the Journal, the Chronicle, or even one of the smaller papers. It was last year, so I don't recall exactly.'

'Do you remember the farmers name?' Where it was? Anything?'

Robert was still digesting the concept of time travel. I grew up with the idea of it. It was envisioned in movies and science. He grew up without electricity or any real technology. He had a lot to process.

'Look, just think about it. Maybe something will come to you tomorrow.' I felt like I had been reborn. Living in this time was something I'd accepted. Now I had hopes of returning to 21. Robert took a coach home and I laid in bed awake all night. I must find my time machine.

It was just before 7:00 the sun was rising and I hadn't slept. Work was the last thing on my mind but I needed my job in case things didn't turn out. When I arrived at the linen shop, Robert was in his office sipping tea.

'Have a seat,' he said.

We both had time to digest my big reveal. Right or wrong I was satisfied with my decision. It relieved my conscience, if nothing else. He poured me a cup of tea from a pot on his desk, 'You gave me so much to think about yesterday.'

I sipped my tea and remained silent.

'I wasn't sure what to believe. The whole thing seemed inconceivable. I saw the money, the cards, the auto license but when you mentioned, Mr. Singer, I knew it to be true.'

'I felt I could trust you.' I said.

'And you can. Just don't mention this to John.'

'You're the only one I've told.'

'So now what happens?' he asked.

'I thought I might search through archives at a library.'

'Library? You need to go to the newspaper's headquarters. They would have archives of their past prints. I know the editor of the, "Claire Chronicle." You could start there. I imagine you're eager to search, but right now you need to focus on the factory. This is an important day and I need you to help set up production line. Matt is loading the wheel carts you requested and will meet us there shortly.'

What I really wanted to do was leave and search every newspaper, but it was important I remain focused and employed in case I couldn't find it.

Robert finished his tea, and stood up, 'Let us go to our factory,' then paused. 'I did remember one thing, from the article. The sheep was found near Ennis.'

Ennis was hours away from Clifden. A long distance for a sheep to walk, let alone one burdened with a heavy load. It should have landed near Clifden where I landed. Our settings were set the same. The whole thing was confusing since I was trying to send us both to Limerick. Robert and I walked to the sewing machine factory. He had endless questions about the future. I started with the basics. Electricity, the light bulb, the radio, TV, telephone, computers, the list went on.

When we arrived at the factory, we set up the carts Matt had constructed. It was a basic assembly line leading from the foundry, and continuing through specially trained crews at each stage of the build. The end of the line would result in one finished sewing machine. We had many bugs to work out and I was fortunate to be focused on keeping the line moving. Everything went reasonably well and I welcomed the distraction.

I left the factory and ran over to the Claire Chronical to search through their archives. After a short introduction, I was led to a large room with stacks of newspapers, organized neatly on shelves, labelled with the months and the years of the prints. There it was, October of 1845. What I was searching for was an illustration of a sheep wearing my time machine and a title, "Steam Engine Sheep." Within an hour I was done. It was fruitless.

I went to Murphy's for a beer and a meal. 'I'll have a Guinness, please.'

'I've already poured it Mr. Ryan. I saw you coming through the door.'

'Do you know where I can get a horse?' I asked.

'You can borrow mine again.'

'I'm going to need to buy one.'

Stephen handed me my beer, 'I have a brother,' he said with a smile. 'He has a farm about a mile past mine on the same road. He'll sell you a horse.'

Another brother, I thought. That explains why there are so many Murphy establishments in my time. It gave me comfort to know his clan had prospered. 'Would I be able to keep the horse at your farm? I'd compensate young Stephen for his time.'

'That won't be a problem. You can discuss the particulars with him.'

There were only half a dozen newspapers within a day's ride from here, but I'd need a horse to see them all. I thanked Stephen, took my beer to a table, ordered a meal, then went back to my room. I was beaming. I felt certain I could find my time machine and get back to 21.

Chapter 12

Archives

Distraction was my only thought. Where was my time machine, and what newspaper was going to lead me to it? I left my place at 7:00 with my saddle on my shoulder and headed to Stephen's brother's farm. It was barely sunrise.

He was out in the barn as I approached, 'Are you Harry? Your brother Stephen told me you could sell me a horse.'

'You're the man that lives in the back of the pub?'

'Yes. I'm Ryan.'

He looked me up and down, 'Let me see your saddle,' he said, as he dragged it off my shoulder. He caressed its surface, and turned it over. 'Nice piece of work.'

'My grandfather made it,' I said proudly.

'Well, let's find a horse that fits it.'

There were twenty horses in the barn and I approached one.

'Nope. Not that one Mr Ryan. I have a few here with a gullet for that saddle.'

I chose a beautiful tanned horse with a symmetrical white strip down her face. Harry put my saddle on her and I rode around the yard. 'She's great. I'll take her.' I paid for the mare, thanked Harry, and rode down to Murphy's farm. Dropping her off with young Stephen, I headed to the sewing machine factory.

The work at the factory was finally bearing fruit. Garth was weeks ahead on producing the smaller pieces, and our steel and iron was starting to catch up. We had treadles and the bodies of sewing machines cast, ready to assemble. They continued down the assembly line, and by days end we had three complete machines. I kept a log and clocked our hours. Each day we worked out the kinks and were establishing a rhythm. By week's end we had completed 22 machines. That was a good first week. My hope was, once we established a flow, we could produce 10 a day.

Robert let me leave early on Saturday. I headed to the Limerick Chronicle, to check their archives. They had a similar set up. Everything was organized, by year and date. It only took an hour, but I came up empty again. Every time I rode somewhere, I would see the effects of the famine. There were crowds of distraught and hungry people walking the roads, with the occasional dead body in the gutter. I wish I could say this was a normal sight, but it never felt normal.

Another week passed, and another ride down a road filled with desperate people, followed by another fruitless search for the illusive, "Steam Engine Sheep." I wasn't overly disappointed. I knew the article existed and a process of elimination would reveal it. Each time I failed, I knew I was checking a box, and getting closer to finding my machine.

Our sewing machine production was accelerating. Most of the kinks were worked out and we were producing 40 machines a week. We had more parts than our production line could handle, so we created a second production line, and hired another crew.

Weeks passed, and I had narrowed down my search. There was one newspaper left on my list. It would definitely have my sheep in it. I went through the October 45 archives but came up short, and felt gutted. There were no other papers distributed in this area. I went back to the pub and drank my sorrows away. Returning to my room, I laid in my bed and pondered. How? We left at the same time but ended up a great distance apart? Perhaps we arrived at different times? Robert recalled the article from last year. Maybe the sheep arrived in September or November? I really didn't understand how it could happen, but I hadn't realized I made a time machine either. Did the weight interfere with the trajectory and the time?

I started my search all over again, going back to "The Claire Chronicle." This time, I searched November and found nothing, then September. There it was, September 7. "The Steam Engine Sheep." I was dancing in circles. I read that article a dozen times. The illustration perfectly matched my machine. The tank of argon gas, the canister of fluids, the battery, all the electronics. I wrote down the particulars. Ennis farmer… Ken Bourke…Larch Hill. I left elated.

When I arrived at the sewing machine factory the following morning, Robert noticed my robustness immediately.

'Good news, I imagine?'

'You bet there is. I found it! I found it!' I was beaming.

'Where?' he asked.

'In Ennis.'

'That's great news. I realize you're eager to get it, but we have a lot of work to accomplish this week. I can give you Saturday off. You can go then.'

'That'll be great. I can't wait to show you my time machine. It's made from plastic, steel, and a metal called aluminium. It'll give you a glimpse of the materials we use in the future.'

Robert's eyes widened. He was enthralled by the knowledge I was sharing with him. Being the only other person that knew about the future, was a special gift and he knew it. I couldn't help but feel great about getting my time machine back. I was conscious of the fact I needed to build a generator, a transformer, and find argon gas. These things did not distract from my happiness. I stayed focused as best I could. We were now producing 70 sewing machines a week, and shipping the majority of them to England. The rest were sold all over Ireland. News was spreading fast.

Saturday arrived. I walked over to the Murphy farm, got my horse, and headed to Ennis. The roads were filled with refugees. It was easy to see the people of Ennis were suffering worse than most. Robert mentioned they had been hit hard with cholera in the 30s. The famine had likely compounded any recovery. When I arrived in Larch Hill, it was evident things were bad. At least half of the shops were closed. The opened ones were clinging to their existence.

I entered a bakery, bought a loaf of bread, and asked the clerk, 'Do you know a farmer named Ken Bourke, the guy who found "The Steam Engine Sheep"?'

'I surely do,' she replied. 'It's a marvel to see.'

'You've seen it?'

'Of course, half the town has. He was charging a penny to see it.'

I followed her directions to his farm. Again, I passed crowds of hungry people. I gave my bread to a reaching hand, and continued onward.

I saw a woman pulling rhubarb, and loading it into baskets. I dismounted and approached her with a huge smile.

'Hello, I'm Ryan. I'm looking for Ken.'

'I'm June, his wife. What would you be needing him for?'

'I wanted to speak to him about his Steam Engine Sheep.'

'It's gone now,' she replied.

I was screaming inside. I could hear the blood pulsing through my temples, 'Gone! Where?'

'You'll need to ask him, he's in the barn,' she said, as she motioned to the left.

Ken was filling a carriage with baskets of rhubarb, cabbage, and cauliflower.

'Hello, I'm Ryan. I'm the owner of the Steam Engine Sheep.'

'I don't have that sheep anymore. I sold it to my neighbour. Nobody came to claim it.'

'I don't care about the sheep. I'm more interested in the apparatus, that was strapped to it. Which neighbour has it?'

'I sold the apparatus to someone else.'

I couldn't control my breathing, and tried to remain calm, 'Who did you sell it to?'

'I don't recall. It was a Spanish fellow.'

'You don't have his name? What did he want it for?'

'He told me he was using it for his show. He did a show with one of those dwarf characters. Like Tom Thumb, from that American circus, but he was Spanish. About knee high,' he said, as he touched the side of his leg.

'Is there anything else you remember? Did he say where he was staying?'

'Nope. He paid me £2 and rode off in his carriage.'

I was distraught. Some Spanish guy with a dwarf was not enough information to help me find it. Inside, I was crying like a baby. There was no way to know where my time machine was. It could be in Spain. I felt guilty. My problems were devastating, but I wasn't suffering like the crowds of people I passed in the country side. I looked at his baskets of vegetables. There was enough food there to feed a village. 'Thanks anyway,' I said, in a defeated tone. 'If you have some sacks for those vegetables, I'll buy them from you.'

'Sure. I have sacks, what would you like?'

'I'll take two sacks of each, I guess. Do you have any cord to tie them together, so I can carry them on my horse?' He filled the sacks, tied them shut, and attached them together in pairs. I paid him, and straddled them over the horse.

'Thanks,' he said, with a smile. 'Wait, he did mention he'd be touring all around the island. He had an act at the Theatre Royal. The one in Dublin, but that was in February.'

'Thank you,' I said, and rode off.

My heart ached as much as it did when I lost my first time machine. I knew deep down it was gone, and so were my chances of getting back. To have such hope given, and taken, was hard to bear. My problems were small compared to the many people out here trying to survive.

I rode a short distance and came upon groups of hungry people, called them over, and started handing out sticks of rhubarb. Suddenly, everyone started running towards me surrounding the horse. It was getting startled and anxious and so was I. There were hands grasping for food. People everywhere reaching out towards me, like a scene from a zombie movie. They were crying out, trying to position themselves closer. I tried to untie another sack, but my horse kept twitching and moving. A man from the crowd pulled out a knife with a long blade, and tried to stab into a sack. He missed, and stabbed my horse. It was happening so fast. The horse reared, I hit the ground hard and was knocked out.

The back of my head was bleeding, when I awoke. Everyone was gone, and so was my horse. I could see a trail of blood on the road, and followed it around the bend. People were tearing violently at my horse. My saddle was covered in blood and cast to the side. It was a terrible scene. As I approached, I could see the remains of my horse. Half of it was gone and two of her legs had been cut off. People were using large stones to break off ribs. A few had knives, cutting off anything they could carry. I broke down in tears. It was painful to watch. I walked over to my bloody saddle, buckled the billet strap, slid it over my head, and carried it on my back.

The long walk home gave me time to think. I was knocked out for a few minutes at best, flush with cash and my silver watch, yet nothing was taken. My saddle was valuable, but all these people needed was a meal. Nothing else had any value.

It was dark by the time I arrived at the pub and I was parched. Scotty and a few men were standing at the bar playing darts.

'Are you all right man?' Scotty asked, 'You're bleeding.'

'It's not my blood,' I touched the back of my head. 'Well, not all of it.'

'Where are they?' Stephen asked. 'We'll straighten them out.'

'It's OK Stephen. It was an accident. I just need a beer.' I put the saddle on the floor and guzzled down half my pint.

89

'So, what happened?' Scotty asked.

I began telling my story... how I was feeding the people, how my horse was stabbed, how it turned into a blood bath. Scotty started laughing.

'It's not funny Scotty!'

'Tis,' he replied. 'Don't get me wrong. It's a sad thing that people are out there suffering and dying, but you did intend to feed them, and you succeeded at that.'

Stephen nodded and smiled in agreement. I ordered another beer and sat at a table. Colleen walked by with plates in her hands and stopped, 'Aren't you a sight, did you run into the moustache from Galway again?'

'It's a long story.'

'I'm sure it is. You'll frighten my customers looking like that. Change your shirt, and clean yourself up, and wash that saddle too, before the blood sets in. I'll have your food ready when you get back.'

I grabbed my saddle and went to the river. I looked at my reflection in the water and realized again, that I may never find my time machine.

Chapter 13

Training Day

Mary had left a letter on my bed, from my young granny. Eviction, hardship, and a bleak Christmas were diverted by my visit. My contribution had reversed their hardship and steered them back to prosperity. In her words, "A Christmas miracle." My existence in this time and my own affluence, was a miracle unto itself. Connecting to my past, and helping them flourish was an amazing opportunity for me. My realization that fate had perhaps imprisoned me here, for a reason. To ensure the future of my family, or to make a difference in this time in some ironic manner.

I responded with kind words, a mutual appreciation of fulfilment, and £60 in paper notes to guarantee them a vigorous future for years to come. Having family in this time enabled me to connect and have some purpose. A reunion rather than an imprisonment. The death of my wife in 2020 was the end of my life there. Perhaps this is my rebirth. I inked out another letter to the "Theatre Royal," enquiring about their "Spanish Dwarf Act," in hopes they had knowledge of their future venues. I didn't pin my hopes on this letter, but saw it more as a lottery of choices. I slept well with a positive new outlook.

John was at the sewing machine factory in the morning. He had good news. A manufacturer in England was going to start producing their version of our sewing machine. They had a larger factory than us, and were considering supplying a world market. We would receive royalties for every machine they built. This was where the real money came in. Robert was going to visit them and discuss terms; introduce them to the Ramson Olds concept of the assembly line that Henry Ford used, and we adopted. John wanted me to go to Galway. A factory there had purchased 10 machines that were in transit, and he wanted me to train the seamstresses. I didn't mind the distraction. After experiencing the loss of my first time machine, I knew distraction was the key to accepting my fate. Business was moving at an astounding rate. Coming from the future enabled me to predict the sewing machine market. They weren't just for manufacturers. They would be in homes all over the world, and I knew it. John had hired 30 more workers for the mill and headed back to train them.

I turned to Robert, 'This is great news.'

'Yes,' he replied. 'Perhaps not as good as you retrieving your time machine.'

'I never got it back. The farmer sold it.'

'I'm sorry to hear that, although I am glad that you're staying. We have prospered immensely since you arrived, and I consider you a good friend.'

'I haven't given up hope. At least 1845 offers me a secure future.' Accepting my life here was not a terrible thing. It pained me to see the suffering, but my new friends were true and honourable.

'So, Robert are you looking forward to returning to Mother England?'

'It's not my only mother, I'm half Irish. I haven't been to England for five years. When I graduated from Trinity, I went back to start a business but the market was saturated, so I came back here and started Feeney's Linens with John.'

'I didn't realize you went to Trinity. I went to Trinity too.'

Robert was shocked, 'Trinity exists in your time?'

'Yes. I spent many years there. I couldn't decide what engineering course I wanted to specialize in, so I started with mechanical engineering, then biomedical and computer, finally settling on electronic engineering. It's a fantastic college.'

Robert smiled, 'Who would have thought we could have almost 2 centuries between us, and still attend the same institution. We are alumni.'

I smiled, 'Yes we are. How cool is that?'

'Very cool,' he replied with a smile.

'I'll need to find a hotel in Galway that has stables, and I'll need a horse!' I blurted.

'I'll need to hire someone to run the shop, since both of us will be gone.'

'What's wrong with Audrey? She's been running it since we opened the new factory, and with twice the staff we used to have. She trained all our new employees.'

'But she's a woman.'

I was getting irritated. 'A qualified person,' I said.

'I'll put an ad in the paper.'

I was pissed. Aside from it being a bad idea, it just pissed me off. If I was going to be living in this time, I wasn't going to stand for this kind of bullshit anymore.

'It has to be Audrey,' I said in defiance.

'But she's a woman. It's just not done.'

'I told you about the future. Women are running the factories during the wars, building cars and airplanes. In my time they make up half the workforce and govern countries. Often better than a man.'

'But she's a…'

'It has to be Audrey,' I insisted, 'I'll only be gone for a week. I will check in on her when I return. We can pay her more to motivate her, and it will still be cheaper than hiring a new supervisor. She's been carrying an added workload for months, and never complained or fell short.'

'Perhaps, I'll consider it,' he said.

'Look, you know it's the smartest choice. You're always telling me how you want to take this company into the future, this also involves a social shift. It may seem unconventional now, but in years to come you will be seen as a trend setter. Other men who did this are remembered in history books. Your name will live on for making such a bold decision.'

He looked at me sternly, then softened his demeanour, 'How much more should I pay her?'

'Lots,' I replied.

Robert smiled, then looked at me queerly, 'What happened to your horse?'

'I'll tell you at lunch.'

It felt good that I could make a difference. If I was going to live in this time, I needed to advocate for others. I needed to take them out of the stone age.

Robert went back to the linen shop to give Audrey the good news. I got to work on our sewing machines. I informed Brett he would be overlooking the entire factory while we were gone, not just the foundry. He had become an asset working the foundry, and understood how the production line functioned. Work kept my mind off my loss and our production was booming. I had scarcely thought about my time machine all day. I had another distraction and stopped by the rectory of a church on my way home, and knocked on the door. A tall man with a soft voice answered, 'Can I help ya?'

'Are you a priest?' I asked.

'Aye I'm Father McGarry. What can I do for ya?'

'Well father, I see you have a Parish Hall. My question is - Is it available to set up as a soup kitchen, and how much would it cost to run... per month?'

'Well, it would only be available four days a week. We use it for other functions. Weddings and such.' He looked up and squinted, 'If we were to set up for the needy in this community, it would take substantial funding. These are trying times, and the needs are great.'

'How much?'

'Let me think... four days a week over a month, it could cost as much as 2 or maybe £3.'

'When would you be able to start?' I asked.

'As soon as I received adequate donations.'

I reached into my pocket, pulled out £3 and handed it to him. He smiled, 'What's your name?'

'I'm Ryan. I'll be back next month, Father. Thank you.'

'God bless you,' he said as I walked away.

Now, I needed to see a man about a horse.

I went home picked up my saddle and headed to Harry Murphy's horse farm. He was riding one of his horses in the field next to his house and rode over when he saw me.

'I expect you're looking for a horse?'

'Yes.'

'Well, Mr. Ryan, let's find you one. I heard about your incident.'

'Yes, it was a good deed that went south.'

'We live in hard times,' he continued.

'Yes. There are so many desperate people and I just wanted to do something to help. It was a poorly executed plan. The horse was wounded by accident and I imagine it fell before it was butchered. You can't blame a hungry man for being desperate.'

'That's the truth.'

He chose a beautiful tan coloured mare with a patch of white on her throat. Saddling her up, I rode her around the yard, 'She's perfect. I'll take her.'

'You know, I have bulls too,' he said with a smile. 'They make a finer meal than a horse, if you decide to do some more charity.'

'I may have to take you up on that,' I replied. I trotted around his field and headed home.

Early the next morning, Audrey greeted me at Feeney's Linens. She was beaming, 'Thank you, sir, for giving me this opportunity.'

'You can thank Robert,' I replied.

'I already did. I know you had a hand in this, and I will prove myself worthy.'

'I never doubted your abilities. You've already proven yourself. I'm very happy your hard work is recognized, and compensated.'

She smiled and nodded.

'Where is Robert?' I asked.

'He's at home making preparations for his trip to England. Mr. Bindon has the instructions for your trip to Galway.'

'Great, I'll go next door to see him. You have a good week Audrey'

'Safe travels Mr. Ryan, and thank you again for everything.'

The mill was loud and active. John was training his new employees on the looms.

'Things are going well here,' I said.

'Exceptional. I couldn't have dreamed we would do so well.'

'That's great! Audrey told me you had my directions to the factory in Galway?'

He handed me a piece of paper, 'I've written everything down. There are directions to the factory and a nearby hotel. We've sent them 10 machines already, and they've ordered 20 more.'

'Who's my contact there?'

'His name is Shane. It's written on the paper.'

'Thanks. I'm riding there now. I'll see you next week.' John returned to his duties, and I got on my horse and headed for Galway.

As I neared Ennis, I could see the remnants of my good deed. It was now just a stain in the road with fragments of fur. Even its hide was used, or boiled for a meal. I continued past fields of potatoes, green and healthy, wondering when they would be stricken by blight. Occasionally a stench would over power me, a blighted crop spreading its curse with the next wind. It was a horrible reminder of what was yet to come.

The devastation was evident in the rural areas, but decreased as I entered the city. There were numerous shuttered businesses, but the city maintained its energy. I visited Galway often in my time.

It was a beautiful vibrant city, with a certain charm. In this time, Eyre Square was a construction site with hundreds of men working. The university had only recently opened its doors, and the landscapers were beautifying the grounds. Track was being laid for a railway, and a station was being erected. It was strange to see such enterprise, amid a famine. The divide of privilege was apparent.

I would be staying in a hotel by the River Corrib, a short walk to the factory where I would be training the seamstresses. It was a beautiful hotel. Modern for its time. They stabled my horse, and checked me in. The room was clean, with brand new Victorian furniture. It was warm and comfortable. There was a picture window overlooking the river, and a washroom down the hall with flush toilets and running water. Comforts that paralleled my time. A far stretch from some of the dank places I'd stayed in the past few months. They even had a restaurant downstairs with a menu, choices not offered at Murphy's pub. I could definitely get used to this.

After breakfast, I walked to the garment factory passing a beautiful home with a carriage out front, and a driver waiting. There was something familiar about it. As my eyes scrutinized the driver, I recognized it was the thug that held me down while Samuel beat me. I pulled up my hood and hurried past, then stopped in the doorway of a building and watched. Fear and excitement consumed me. I felt an impulse to do something, but stayed hidden for several minutes. My eyes fixed on Samuel as he came out of the house, wearing my coat. It wasn't as though I didn't deserve some payback for selling him a bad Apple, but he should have been happy with the money he stole. It was 5 times what I had taken from him, yet he still took my coat. I wanted to run up and rip it off his shoulders, but I just stood there as he got into the carriage and drove off.

I was angry at myself, thinking, I coulda, shoulda… It left me with nothing but regret. There was truly nothing I could do. I regained my composure before entering the factory, and introduced myself to Shane. He escorted me onto the factory floor. It dwarfed Feeney Linens. The crew was made up of women and children, and they sat quietly as Shane introduced me. They had unpacked the sewing machines we delivered, and arranged them in a row. I picked out nine workers and began my training session.

Much the same as Feeney's Linens, there were far more workers than machines. After hours of instruction, I left them to sew a garment.

I had the mechanics gather around the 10th sewing machine. They were skilled at repairing everything in the factory. Each one practiced disassembling and reassembling it. This went on for the remainder of the day.

As the sun set, I walked back to the hotel past Samuel's house. It haunted me all day seeing him wearing my coat. His carriage was parked in the coach house attached to his home, with no sign of his thug driver. I wanted to do something. Break a window. Damage his carriage. Anything. Instead, I just continued and let rage consume me.

Each morning I'd pass that bastard's house, and his thug would be sitting out front waiting for him. I'd stand hooded in a doorway watching with regret. On Sunday the factory was closed, but I had 2 more training sessions to fulfil. I made my way over to Samuel's house to survey the situation. By half past seven, I gave up and explored the city for a few hours, then returned to Samuel's and spied some more. I was obsessed.

A woman and two teenage girls were getting into the carriage, and Samuel was driving. He wasn't wearing my coat, and there was no sign of his thug either. As he rode off, I ran behind him for several blocks. The noise of the hoofs and wheels drowned out the sound of me panting, and there were no rear-view mirrors. I gave up my chase. I felt so powerless and violated the night he beat me down. I wanted payback, although I had no real plan.

Monday morning the rain was pelting down, on my way to the factory. As I walked past Samuel's house, he was exiting his home, wearing my coat. I hid in a doorway and watched him get into the carriage as his thug drove; then ran behind, following as they wove through the streets. He stopped a few hundred metres ahead of me and I continued towards him. The rain stopped and the sun poured out from behind the clouds. I could see the blurred image of Samuel standing outside of the carriage with my coat on. He removed it, threw it in the back and shut the door, then entered a nearby building. As I got closer, I could see his thug sitting in the driver's seat having a smoke in front of an abandoned building, with a stone wall around it. It was next to a whore house.

Who goes to a whore house at half past seven in the morning? I needed to distract him somehow, then grab my coat. I put on my hood and walked over to the wall in front of the carriage. It was over a meter high with chained gates.

With my back to the coach, I reached into my pocket and pulled out a handful of coins, then in a disguised voice I said, 'Screw you bitch,' and tossed a penny at the abandoned building. The thug chuckled behind me. I threw another penny, then another. The carriage springs squeaked as he stepped down. I tilted my head away as he approached the wall, then threw a handful of coins at the building. He dragged himself over that wall with great effort. My adrenaline was pumping. This was it. I ran to the carriage and tried the door. It was locked. The thug had his head down looking for coins.

I jumped in the driver's seat released the break and rode off with the carriage. My head felt like it was going to explode. The thug was still struggling to get back over the wall. There was no fear, just vindication. Several blocks later, I stopped in front of a stretch of abandoned buildings. I reached in the other door and grabbed my coat. My eyes darted quickly around the street. It was empty. Removing the breast collar from the horses, I set them free, then walked briskly back to my hotel. I could scarcely breathe as laughter robbed me of each breath. Returning to my hotel, I stowed my trophy, changed my clothes, and bought a hat on my way to the factory.

It felt great! Invigorating! Work was a pleasure and I relished the karma I inflicted on that prick. On my last trip to the factory, I walked past Samuel's house. Hidden under my hat, I chuckled at his empty coach house. No carriage or horses.

I couldn't get out of Galway fast enough. Putting as much distance between me and Samuel was all that mattered. I was mindful not to wear my prize. I wore my hat and jumper until I was out of town, then put on my linen coat. Wearing the yellow one would be risky. I'd never be able to wear it again. It didn't take long to pick up the scent of blight and the sight of the refugees slowed me to a trot. Abandoned buildings were converted into food depots, giving out Indian corn from America. The locals and the paper called it "Peel's Brimstone." This was the relief, prime minister, Robert Peel provided. The Irish didn't know what to do with it and they didn't have the equipment to process it into flour. It was too hard to chew, and a solution too hard to swallow. I passed more green fields of potatoes, followed by a whiff of rotten blight. This year's crop failure would bring on "Black 47." The worst was still to come.

Chapter 14

Full Steam Ahead

The cities I visited were always prosperous. They seemed less blighted by the blight. Shops were closed and beggars visible, but I never saw a body lying in the streets. Industry seemed to carry on, yet the rural communities always suffered the most. A class system that deemed them unworthy of humanity. Not unlike today, where our consumption coupled with the hoarding of billions, cedes poverty, war, and famine in developing countries. Our greed empties the bottom shelf, whether its outside our city walls or outside our continent. History does repeat itself. It was a sad realization that has perpetuated for generations. Our choice of victims in 21 is further from our shores and somehow further from our conscience. As I crossed the bridge into my city, the extreme poverty melted away.

I stabled my horse at Murphy's farm and went home to rest. My bright yellow coat hung on the wall, and I admired it like the trophy that it was. The power taken from months ago had been restored.

Bright and early, I headed to Feeney's Linens. Audrey was cheerful. She looked up from her work and walked over to greet me.

'Hello Audrey, how was your first week?'

'Just grand, we're reaching our quotas, and the sewing machines make work enjoyable.'

'Good to hear. If you need anything, I'll be over at the sewing machine factory.'

She returned to work, and I headed to the factory. I didn't really need to check on her but I told Robert I would.

The sewing factory was loud, hot, and productive. I was greeted by Brett as I entered.

'Good morning, sir. How was your trip?'

'Brilliant. They've learned how to use the sewing machines and they're ready for 20 more.'

'We're loading 10 as we speak, and shipping them out today.'

'That's just great Brett, we're lucky to have you.'

We had so many orders for machines, we couldn't fulfil them fast enough. I glanced around the factory, 'Is Robert back yet?'

'No sir, but the solicitor that travelled with him has returned, and he left you a note in the office. I best get back to work.'

I entered the office and read the note. Robert was staying to help with the assembly line and would return in a few days. I was instructed to have 2 zipper dies made for a British company that was manufacturing copies of our sewing machines. This meant they would be producing our zippers as well, and paying us royalties.

My life here was good. It wasn't 2021, but it was as good as anyone could ask for, in this time. The reality was, the only problems I had were luxury problems. Having wealth in this time wasn't anything like 21. What do you buy with it? A second horse or carriage. A piano. All I really wanted was a new mattress.

I passed a furniture store on my way home, and ordered a new mattress. Although I liked my shabby quarters at the Murphy's, the comfort I'd experienced at the hotel made me realize I needed an upgrade. If I was going to be stuck here in this time, I should be comfortable.

My plan was to buy a farm. I had accumulated enough wealth to purchase one now. The future would deliver several farms at famine prices. I knew that once 1847 hit, the English land owners would be losing their tenants and dumping their land for pennies on the dollar. Many were losing them already. My stay at the Murphy's was a calculated decision. I wanted to buy all the land I could afford, and lease all the lots for a fraction of the price the farmers were paying now. This would help many families survive the famine. Money wouldn't be a factor once my royalties started rolling in.

Stephen greeted me with his usual smile.

'I'll have a Guinness please.'

'It's already poured Mr. Ryan. I saw you coming through the door. It'll take a minute to settle.'

'Thank you, Stephen.'

'How was your trip?' he asked.

'It was great. I got all my work done and picked up a coat on the way out.'

'Splendid,' he replied, then handed me my beer.

'Hey Stephen?' I asked, 'I bought a new mattress. They're delivering it tomorrow. I wanted to know where to dispose of the old one.'

'Wait,' he said, as he turned his head, 'Colleen!'

Colleen came out of the kitchen.

Stephen addressed her, 'Mr. Ryan here is getting a new mattress tomorrow and wants to know where to put the old one.'

Colleen approached me, 'What happened to your mattress?'

'Nothing. It's just old and stained with blood.'

'Did you turn it over?'

'Um. No. Um. I bought a new one, so I just want to know where to dump the old one?'

'Dump?' she said, with a queer look on her face. 'Mary can scrub out the stains and you can just turn it over. It's a perfectly good mattress, it's not even 10 years old.'

'Well,' I said. 'The new one's coming tomorrow, so…'

'I won't be lecturing you how you squander your money,' she uttered. 'I'll find a place for your mattress.'

She went back to the kitchen, and I stood at the bar talking to Stephen.

Stephen smiled, 'People are really liking the dart panel you made. Scotty has been teaching them the rules. I shoot a few games too, when it slows down.'

'Dart board…' I replied. I'm glad you like it. It's fairly popular where I come from.'

A game of darts was a great pass time. It wasn't like you could watch a match on TV. I made a mindful effort to embrace the simpler things. This was going to be my new life, and brooding about it would only be self-destructive. I missed my phone less, appreciated a hand written letter more, and felt I was adjusting to the slower pace quite well. I didn't have much of a choice, but I felt centred here just the same.

What was I really missing? A hollow text? A self-endowed gift from Amazon? An envied post from someone, that didn't invite me to their night out? Was I really missing anything in 21, other than friends and family?

I focused on work. I visited the linen shop every morning, then headed to the sewing machine factory, then to the Black Smith shop, to help Garth assemble the parts of the zipper dies. At night I'd spend time in my room enjoying my new mattress, and admiring the coat I would never be able to wear.

A letter arrived from "Theatre Royal," in Dublin. My last hope. My windfall.

It read:

"Dear Mr. McCullough;

In answer to your query regarding "Miguel the Dwarf and his Steam Engine Sheep," he had left our venue in February, but will be returning. We welcome you to enjoy his return performances, July 13th, and 14th. Tickets can be purchased at our booth outside the venue, Monday – Sunday. We look forward to your patronage.

Sincerely......"

Sincerely? It's the 18th! When is the phone going to be invented? Where do they play next? Why does the mail take so long? Comedy and tragedy. My time machine is lingering on this island! Why can't I get an answer that doesn't take 2 weeks? Feck! Time was an evil tormentor. I was angry and frustrated. I penned another letter, requesting locations and dates of ALL the future venues. I knew I would remain in limbo for a few more weeks.

I poured myself into work, assembling the parts of the zipper dies, then drank heavily almost every night. Hard work, alcohol, and self-pity. I was getting my work completed but numbing my thoughts. After a few days of abuse, Robert came back from England. It was nearing the end of the day, and he came bearing gifts.

'How was your trip?' I asked.

'Fruitful. I don't know where to start?'

'Start at the beginning,' I said.

'Well, they have three furnaces and triple our capacity. We could stop production now, and never have to work again; with the royalties we will get from this one factory. I toured almost a dozen more while I was there, and they all sparked an interest. You were right about the growth of the sewing machine.'

'I had some inside information,' I replied. 'I knew where the market would take it.'

'You did indeed,' he said with a smile. 'I think I have a sense of how you feel, knowing the outcome of the future. What you told me about the sewing machine being used worldwide, put me in a place of certainty. As though my sales were predetermined by history. A powerful clairvoyance.'

I didn't care about any good news. Money wasn't going to make me happy right now.

'Knowing the future does have its benefits.' I said. 'The downside is, you also know the cynical outcome as well. The inevitable wars, genocide, famine, and atrocities that mankind is going to unleash.'

Robert paused, 'Stop your malcontent. This is glorious news.'

'I'm sorry. You're right. It hasn't been a good week for me.'

'Problems in Galway?'

'No. Galway was a blast. I even got my yellow coat back.'

I told Robert every detail of how I stole the carriage, and liberated the horses. He couldn't stop laughing and it made me feel a bit better.

'That is an exceptional escapade,' he said. 'There's no reason you need be so melancholy.'

'You're right,' I laughed. 'But I'll never be able to wear that coat again. That's the good news. The bad news is, my time machine was in Dublin just a few days ago, and I missed my chance to get it back.'

Robert smiled as though he were pleased with my loss, 'Perhaps another opportunity will arise,' he said, as he pulled a scrap of paper from his vest pocket. 'Perhaps on July 23rd at the Theatre Royal, in Waterford. Or the 24th.

I had no idea what he was talking about.

'I know how you must feel my friend, but there is good news. I saw bulletins posted in London about "Miguel the Dwarf and his Steam Engine Sheep," but I missed the act by mere hours. I was hoping to purchase your time machine on your behalf. I did however get notice of his appearance at the Theatre Royal in Dublin and in Waterford, which is yet to debut.'

'You're kidding?'

'I kid you not,' he replied with a grin.

This was it. I really felt this was it. This time I would get my time machine back, 'Thank you, thank you, thank you. This is amazing. I don't know what to say?'

'Perhaps thank you, might be appropriate,' he said in jest, then handed me the piece of paper.

'July 23rd. I can't believe it?'

'I suspect you'll be absent from work for the next few days?'
'I'd leave tonight if I could trust my horse in the dark,' I replied.
'I have to go. I have to get ready.'
I gave Robert a hug. He seemed genuinely happy for me. Nothing was going to stop me from getting my time machine this time.

Chapter 15

Take Your Time

Sitting by the flickering candle light, I reminisced about my past in the future and my time here. My quest to return to 21 had consumed so much of my time and effort, I had overlooked what I would be leaving in the past. An environment untainted by progress. The friends I had made. The family I had met. I would never see them again. All the people that had become such an important part of my life, would be history. The experiences I've had here, although often tragic, had surpassed anything in my life. It was a test of survival at so many levels. A growth, no other person but a time traveller could experience. A full spectrum of emotions. My time here would be lost to memory.

Excited and nervous, I spent the night packing my saddle bags for Waterford, and rehearsing my meeting with the Spanish dwarf. How would I proposition him for my time machine? I played out a dozen scenarios in my mind until the morning sun broke my concentration, and lit my path out of Doonass.

Each time I left my city, my optimism was paralyzed by the anguish I witnessed along the road. It was unavoidable. The smell was piercing. Rotting blight dominated the air. Broken families wandered the roads in search of hope. I carried my privilege like an anchor. The guilt I felt was constant.

A half day of riding brought me to Waterford and the Granville Hotel. A familiar building. It was the closest hotel to the Theatre Royal. I had stayed here in 2018 and was curious to see how it had changed. As I rode up, I saw a colourful carriage parked out front. A banner painted on the side read, "Miguel the Dwarf and his Steam Engine Sheep." There was a tiny man, a sheep, and my time machine painted in bright colours. The front of the carriage had a driver's seat, with a trunk and luggage on the roof, and a cab beneath. I peered into the windows. It was empty. The back of the carriage had a separate cage for the sheep.

As I climbed in the driver's seat, a large man came running out of the hotel, 'Get down!' he shouted.

I stepped down as he approached. He was angry and aggressive, 'Get away from there!'

'I want to see the show tonight,' I said.

He pointed towards the theatre, 'You can get tickets at the box office!'

'Who are you?' I asked.

'None of your business, who I am! Get away from the carriage!'

I stepped away, crossed the street, and watched as he handed the luggage down to the hotel porter, who followed him inside. The trunk remained on the roof of the carriage, and likely held my time machine. Within a few minutes he exited the hotel, got in the driver's seat, and drove the carriage down the street. I followed him as he stopped in front of the Theatre Royal, entered through a side entrance, then returned with a crew and unloaded the trunk and the sheep. That trunk seemed heavy, which meant it could only be one thing. My time machine.

I sat and waited for him to leave, then bought a ticket at the booth, for the show. I'd have to wait for tonight to make my proposal. I was nervous but excited, and went back to the Granville Hotel to book a room.

The hotel clerk was pleasant, 'Is this your first time at The Granville?'

'No. I was here a few years ago.'

'Well, welcome back.'

I looked at the wall behind his desk. There were pigeon holes for mail and messages. There was a glass case with skeleton keys, 'I'm here with the Spanish Dwarf act,' I said. 'Do you know what room they are staying in?'

He paused and glanced at his book, 'Room 17. There's no adjacent room, but I can give you room 21 down the hall if you like.'

'Splendid,' I replied. 'What about my horse? It's right out front.' He signalled a porter to take my horse, and handed me a numbered tag for the stable stall. I watched as he pulled my key from the glass case. I noted there were extra keys on my hook.

I admired the hotel lobby on the way to my room. The furniture was of the Georgian era. Antiques of this time, yet quite beautiful. There was a communal bathroom down the hall. The design was completely different from 2018, but it had the same warmth I remembered.

My pursuit to get here had left me completely unprepared. The sheep's time machine was heavy, and I should have brought a cart to carry it back. Now, I would need to tie it to my horse, and walk it back to Doonass. I asked the front desk for directions to a general store, and purchased some rope. All I needed to do now was buy back my time machine, tie it to my horse and head home. My enthusiasm was percolating. I lingered in my room anticipating my reward, anxious to be reunited with my time machine, then left for the show.

Sitting three rows from the stage in the theatre gave me a perfect view. It was a terrible act. Insulting to the dwarf, yet cheered on by the crowd. A sign of the times. In the second act the dwarf rode in on a cart. It was led by a sheep wearing my time machine. Steam whistle sound effects were piped in from back stage, and an incense canister hung from the cart. I was quivering inside. There it was, in plain sight. My time machine. Everything went quiet in my mind. A salty scent of church incense burned. Muffled laughter, cheers and clapping, hummed in the background. My only focus was analysing my machine, its parts and condition. It was missing the umbilical lines. The tank was damaged. The computer was tied shut. I just needed it in my possession, and I could deal with the repairs.

When the show ended, I waited patiently for the audience to clear, took a deep breath, and headed backstage. There was no sign of the sheep or my machine, just a small group of people.

As I approached the Dwarf, the driver blocked my path. He recognized me from earlier in the day.

'You,' he said. 'Go away.'

'Miguel!' I cried. 'I want to buy your time ma.... steam engine.'

He smiled and pointed to his manager, 'no englais.'

I turned to his manager, 'My name is Ryan. I want to buy your steam engine.'

He smirked and said, 'Not to sell.'

'I will pay £4,' I cried.

'No! Not for sell.'

'£10,' I belted out.

'Not for sell,' he repeated.

I stepped closer, 'You have to sell it to me. It's my machine!'

The driver grabbed me by the shoulder, 'Get out!' he demanded.

I resisted. I had to get it back. He cradled me in a bear hug, pushed me down the hallway, and out the side exit.

'Go!' he demanded as he dropped me on my ass in the alley, and slammed the door.

Waiting outside, I concealed myself behind empty crates and checked my watch. My mind was racing. The door finally opened, and I watched them leave. The machine was still inside. I circled the building and double checked the doors. It was a sealed vault. I was distraught and disheartened. I was not going to let that time machine get away from me. My mind plotted a ridiculous plan on my way back to the hotel. I sat at the bar and gazed at the lobby. There was one clerk at the desk and two hotel porters. I sized them up. The youngest porter was my target. He had the worst shoes and I hoped he could be compromised.

I sat, drank, and summed up the courage, then motioned him over.

'What's your name son?' I asked.

'Jimmy.'

'Jimmy? Really?'

'No,' he replied, 'It's actually Henry, but everyone just calls me Jimmy so I....'

'Well Jimmy, how would you like to make a pound?'

'A pound, sir? How?' he asked in amazement. A pound was likely 2- or 3-months wage for him.

'The dwarf in room 17 has taken something that belongs to me.'

'I can get the manager,' he replied.

'No need Jimmy. He's an old friend, and we play these games everywhere we travel. So, I want to take it back, and at our next performance, he will muse me in a similar way. You, see?'

Jimmy looked at me with a blank expression on his face.

'So, Jimmy, what I need from you is one of those extra keys for room 17, and I will give you this gold coin.'

I waved a gold coin in front of him like a carrot.

'No sir, I can't do that. I could lose my job.'

I was desperate, 'It's all in good fun Jimmy. We do this to each other all the time. At every hotel we stay in. We're good friends.'

Jimmy looked at the coin and over his shoulder, 'Nobody will know sir?'

'No. It'll never lead back to you. It's all in good fun.'

Jimmy kept looking around.

'Take your time,' I said. 'Room 17. I'll be sitting right here

109

having drinks.'

I sat and waited and sipped my drink. Jimmy seemed scared and was losing his courage. I looked at him, then approached the front desk. I asked the clerk to come to the entrance door, then nodded at Jimmy.

The clerk approached me, 'Can I help you sir?'

'Yes,' I replied, as I pointed to a store across the street, 'What is that building there? With the awning?'

I turned back to Jimmy and gave him a nod to grab the key.

'Which one sir?' asked the clerk.

'The white one.'

'That's the fish monger, sir.'

'Is it fresh?'

'Yes, every day sir.'

Jimmy grabbed the key and smiled.

'Thank you for your time,' I said and I went back to the bar.

He waited a few minutes and returned with the key, and received his reward. I finished my drink and headed to my room. I wasn't sure what I was going to do with it, but if that time machine made it back to the room after tomorrow's show, I was going to take it regardless of the consequences.

I spent the next day wandering around the city, not really sightseeing, but plotting out a plan in my head while trying to burn off my pent-up anxiety. As evening fell, I sat at a café sipping tea and staring at my watch. I strolled, past the theatre after the show, and waited. The sheep was walked out and caged in the back of the carriage. Two stage workers loaded the chest with the time machine. I followed them down the block to the hotel, and watched them unload the chest and carry it to their room. Slipping into my room, I sat by the door. Faint cries of laughter, and the clinking of glasses travelled down the hallway. My patience was being tested. There was nothing I could do but wait, and hope they would leave their room. Over an hour passed as I sat by my door listening.

Finally, the door opened, and I heard their footsteps as they passed my room. I peeked out. The driver, the manager, and the dwarf, walked past. My heart was pounding so hard it was bruising my ribs. I wasted no time. I took my key and dashed down the hallway, opened the door, and saw the trunk sitting in front of me in the dark. It was locked. I felt around the dresser and heard the

110

cling of a spoon in a bowl, grabbed it, and pried open the chest.
There it was, barely visible. My time machine.

My adrenaline was pumping. I lugged it out of the trunk, closed
the lid and carried it back to my room. Running back, I threw £2
on the dresser and locked the door. Fear took over, and I needed
to act fast. I dashed to the stables, and handed the keeper the tag
for my horse. He seemed to take forever to saddle her and finally
came out. Every minute seemed like an hour, and I needed to get
out of Waterford quickly.

The window to my room was in the back just outside the stable,
so I walked my horse over, then ran back inside and began stuffing
everything in my saddle bags. Nothing was more important than
this moment. I opened my window, threw the rope and my saddle
bags out, teetered the time machine on the window ledge, and
jumped down. I pulled the horse close, then lugged that mass on
its back and began tying it on.

A light sparked 2 rooms over. Room 17. I continued tying the
time machine to my horse. It was so heavy. The moonless night
was in my favour, but the streets were lit with torches. I heard a
cry from room 17, then jumped on my horse and rode. Everything
was happening in slow motion. I moved out to the street and
someone shouted, 'Landron! Police! Police!' The horse was
weighed down with me and my time machine. I rode as hard as I
could, then I heard a whistle.

'Stop!'

'Stop!'

Again I heard the whistle, but continued frantically towards the
darkness at the edge of town. A cloak. I could hear the panting
breath from my horse, and feel the heat coming from her body,
then the sound of the Irish Constabulary in pursuit. I thought of
nothing else but reaching the abyss at the edge of town. I kicked
that horse hard, oblivious of her load. This was my deciding
moment. My time. My future.

Suddenly, I was engulfed in darkness and riding blind. The
whistle from the Irish Constabulary was fading. Their gallop went
silent. I was free and I could feel it, until I was thrown to the
roadside in the pitch black of night. Down on the ground, I
crawled over to quiet my horse. There was only heat coming from
her body. She was motionless. Feck! I laid beside her and listened
to the police in the distance. They were talking, and they lingered

for several minutes. I could scarcely breathe. My horse was dead, so I sat quietly in the dark. I waited and listened for the voices to disappear.

The police rode back to town. Fearing it was a trick to draw me out to the road, I stayed hidden without moving. I was so afraid of getting caught. My chances of getting back to 21 would certainly be extinguished. I untied my time machine from the carrion and dragged it deep into the bushes, then retrieved my saddle and saddle bags.

I changed my clothes, grabbed my scissors that I used to trim my beard, and began cutting it to the flesh. I walked back to town cutting my hair almost to the scalp. It was dark but I took mental notes of all the bends in the road as I passed, while cutting away my identity. Nervously entering the town, I looked for any coach that would take me to Doonass. There was a carriage man outside of a pub.

'Can you give me a lift to Doonass,' I asked.

He looked me in my hairless disguise. I must have looked a mess.

'No,' he replied.

'Why not?'

'Because you don't look as though you could pay and you're probably the man the IC we're chasing earlier.'

The Irish Constabulary had certainly tagged me.

'How much would you charge?'

He looked at me and smirked, 'I'd have to charge you 5 shillings to get there, 5 shillings for my empty ride back and 5 more my trouble.'

Highway robbery. Twenty shillings in a pound.

'I'll give you a pound right now if you'll take me.'

He put out his hand and I handed him a pound, 'Get in.'

'I'll need to stop a few minutes up the road and retrieve my saddle and my belongings.'

'Tell me where.' he replied.

We rode out of town, and I watched every bend in the road.

'OK,' I said. 'Right here.'

I heaved my machine into the carriage, followed by my saddle. The oil lamp from the carriage illuminated the corpse of my horse a few meters up the road.

The carriage man shouted, 'Rode her to death, did ya. That won't go to waste. It'll be gone by daybreak.'

I took a deep breath. Then analysed my time machine. It was damaged even more since the fall. I needed to get it to Doonass, repair it, and get home.

Chapter 16

Time Served

The sun began to rise as we entered Doonass. My anxiety consumed me as I lugged my time machine onto the stoop in front of my door, then went back to the carriage for my saddle and saddle bags. The emotion was intense. After getting everything into my room I immediately assessed the damage. The fall from the horse completely flattened my fluid tank that hooked up to the intravenous line, which was also gone. The electronics and computer needed some mending, but were in good shape. I was relieved nothing was beyond repair. Everything else was moderately damaged but could be restored or replaced. Overall, with some work I would be able to fix it and get back to 21.

I wasted no time and headed to the black smith shop. Garth was just opening.

'Good morning, Garth, how's everything?'

'Busy as usual,' he replied. He looked me straight in the eyes, 'What happened to you? I barely recognised you.'

'I'm not very good at grooming myself,' I replied with a smile. 'I guess I'll need to visit the barber and have him clean me up.'

I handed him my flattened stainless-steel tank, 'I need you to make me another tank like this.'

Garth caressed the flattened steel like it was a precious metal, 'What is this?'

'It was a tank.'

'What kind of metal is this?'

'It's stainless steel.'

He continued to stroke it, 'It's beautiful. I had no idea such a substance existed.'

It seems stainless steel has yet to be invented, 'It's an alloy made of iron, chromium, nickel, and silica, with some carbon. I need you to make me a new one. I also want some tubes, a rod and a needle made from it as well.'

Garth seemed excited about this new material, 'I can melt this down, but I'd need more of this to produce all the parts you require. I don't have chromium. I don't even know where to acquire it. I do have nickel, and I can get silica. I would need to know the proportions.'

I wasn't sure of the exact proportions, but I did know there was about 70 % iron 20% chromium and minute quantities of the other elements. It was imperative that my fluid tank was made from stainless steel, as iron would oxidise with the chemicals I added to the solution, and have adverse effects on my IV feed.

'I will find you some chromium,' I said. 'Do you have copper or gold?'

'Sure, I have copper,' he replied. 'But no gold.'

'Can you make some thin gauge copper wire? I'd need about 1500 yards to start, and about 2 yards of gold wire.' I reached into my pocked and pulled out £2 in gold. 'You can use these for the gold wire. I'll draw up plans for the other parts and get them to you.'

Garth took the coins. That would get him started. My generator and transformer would need other parts, but at least things were moving forward. I had to look a bit more presentable, before I went to the sewing machine factory to give Robert the good news

I headed to the barber for some hygienic rehab. My young barber was still there. He was my first barber, in this time and a great source of the news of the times.

'Hello sir,' I said. 'How are you?'

'Fine. What can I do for you?'

'I need you to fix the damage I caused. I think I'll have a clean shave this time.'

'Have you been here before?'

'Yes, I was here about a year ago. I had a yellow coat.'

'Ah yes, I remember you well. I didn't recognise you with everything cut the way it is.'

He put the kettle on the stove, sat me down, and began cutting.

'How have you been?' I asked.

'Well sir, it's been a tough couple of months.'

'Is business slow?'

'No business is good,' he replied. 'It's my family and the farm.'

'I'm sorry, I won't pry.'

'It's fine, I've repeated this story several times. It seems to make it easier to accept.'

I stared at him through the mirror and listened. It must have been therapeutic for him to talk about it.

'My father planted his potato crop in March, as he always had. It was growing green and strong until June, then it got the blight. It spread right through the entire field. In a fortnight it became a rotten foul mass.'

'That's horrible,' I said.

'It certainly was, he barely recovered from the blight we had last year. This one proved too much for him. He was facing eviction and hung himself from a tree on the property.'

My heart sunk. I'm sure this scenario is playing out all over the country. Another sad reality of the times.

'I'm so sorry to hear it,' I said. 'What about your mother?'

'I have a flat in town, she lives with me now.'

This is the life that so many people would bear in this time. It has been my curse from the beginning, knowing how history will play out. I suffered from survivor's guilt, yet hadn't really suffered at all. He was my reality check coming into this time, and now going out. I left there with a clean new look, and a reminder that the worst was yet to come. Black 47 was approaching, and this year's blight would yield its powerful blow.

When I arrived at the sewing machine factory, it was boiling over with production. Robert was startled as I entered the office. He jumped out of his seat, 'Well, well, well,' he said. 'I didn't recognise you. Is this the way people groom themselves in the future?'

'This is the way time machine thieves conceal their identity,'

Robert smiled, 'Did you get it?'

'I sure did!'

I proceeded to fill him in on every detail. He was locked into my every word.

'When do you leave?' he asked.

'Not for some time, I need to make repairs and build an electric generator. I can power it from the mill wheel, if that's OK with you?'

'Whatever you need.'

There was so much help I needed. If I was going to repair it rapidly.

'When you attended Trinity, did you study chemistry?' I asked.

'Certainly, it was the knowledge I needed for the fabric industry, dying, bleaching, we studied all 58 elements.'

116

I was stunned, '58 elements in the periodic table?'

'I'm not sure about the period table, but we studied 58 elements. Are there more elements in the future?'

'Yes. There are 118 in 2021. We refer to the group of elements as the periodic table.'

Robert seemed shocked.

'Have you heard of chromium or argon gas?' I asked.

'Chromium does sound familiar, and we've known about argon gas for some time.'

What a relief. My future was held in the balance of these 2 elements, 'That's fantastic. Do you know where can I find chromium and argon gas?'

Robert looked at me with a disappointed brow, 'I can make some enquiries for chromium, but argon is a known element, but unattainable.'

That was terrible news. Argon gas was vital for my time machine. I obtained it from a welding supplier in 21. There was no place to purchase it here. Making it myself wouldn't be a problem in my time, but here and now was a different story. I would need a proper laboratory to produce it. I'd need a fractional distillation apparatus and minerals. I picked Robert's brain for any information he could provide. It was very disappointing to come this far and hit a wall.

Robert could see my desperation, 'I can introduce you to my chemistry professor in Dublin. If that would help.'

'Maybe I could use his lab.' I asked.

'I can write a letter. With your knowledge, he would certainly let you use his laboratory. You could provide him with much insight.'

That's exactly what I needed. With 58 elements, and no periodic table yet established, perhaps I could be an asset to this professor and in turn get what I need. 'If you could do that for me Robert, I would be forever in your debt.'

Robert smiled, 'I'll send out a letter of introduction tomorrow.'

This gave me a certain amount of relief. I'm not sure how well equipped a laboratory in this time would be. It certainly lacked elements. 'Write this down,' I said. 'These are the things I need you to ask your professor for, in the letter.'

Robert took his fountain pen and steadied it over a sheet of paper.

'Ask him if he can acquire chromium, carbon, and lodestone. I also need to know if he has any knowledge of fractional distillation. Ask if he has calcium or magnesium and a nitride. Um... I can't think... that will do for now. If I think of anything else, I'll let you know.'

'Now, I'd like to see that machine of yours,' he said.

We headed to Murphy's. I was so excited to show him my time machine. My heart sunk as we approached the pub. There were 2 Irish Constabulary horses tied out front with badges on the saddles. I knew they were there for me. I registered with this address at the hotel. I never planned to steal it at the time.

I looked at Robert and pointed to the horses, 'I'm screwed. They're here for me.'

Not only would I lose my time machine, I would lose my freedom, 'I can't go in,' I said.

'We must!' he replied. 'We are men of means and stature. We will address this.'

This was terrible. I wanted to run away. I couldn't go anywhere without my time machine.

Robert saw the fear in me, 'Look, we will address this. I am well connected in this city. We have one of the best barristers available. You will need to steady yourself.'

'Ok,' I said. 'Let's do this.'

We stepped into Murphy's pub and the 2 cops were speaking with Stephen and Colleen. I took a deep breath and put on my best face. I had no idea what they were told. My only plan was to lie to them, and hope. Colleen and Stephen glared at me as I entered. The IC turned to me, then turned back.

Colleen gestured to me, 'This is Mr. Ryan.'

One of the cops looked me up and down. He may have been the one chasing me, but it was hard to tell.

'Are you Ryan McCullough?' he asked.

'Yes.'

'Do you own a tanned coloured horse?'

'No.'

I had been lying about my identity for almost a year, and I knew not to try too hard and keep my answers brief.

'Where were you yesterday?'

'I was here. What's this about, officer?'

'It seems somebody has been trying to impersonate you. A scruffy man with sandy brown hair and a beard. Do you know anyone that fits that description?'

'No.'

Robert chimed in, 'I'm Robert Feeney, I'm the owner the linen factory, Mr. McCullough here, is one of my employees.'

The cop turned to Robert, 'It seems a man booked a room in the Granville hotel in Waterford using the name Ryan McCullough, and registered with this address, then stole a prop from a theatre act.'

Stephen and Colleen listened intensely.

'I can assure you Mr. McCullough has been working here all week. He is an esteemed employee. This is nothing short of harassment!' Robert trumpeted.

'I apologise sir, but we are required to investigate. He clearly is not the man I was chasing yesterday, and it appears everyone here has affirmed his alibi. I am required to ask these questions.'

'Well then,' Robert said. 'Now that his whereabouts have been established, perhaps you need to focus your investigation closer to home.'

'Perhaps,' he replied.

The cop turned to his partner, 'I think we are done here.'

His partner nodded. I felt a huge sigh of relief. His partner looked at me and said, 'We will just need to inspect your premises and we can close this investigation.'

Feck!

My heart hit the ground. They would find the time machine, and expose my lies. I would certainly do prison time for this, even with the best lawyers.

Colleen turned to the cops, 'I have his key here,' she said. 'Follow me.'

She led them out to the courtyard, and Robert and I followed. I was gutted and scared. I'd never survive in a prison in this time, or my own. We walked towards my room, then right past it to Scotty's door. Colleen unlocked the door and let the IC enter. They glanced quickly into the room, while holding their noses.

One of them asked, 'What's that smell?'

'It's bleaching agent for the linen,' I replied.

Robert interrupted, 'Ryan is a supervisor for our bleaching crew.'

The police looked at each other, then turned to me, 'Thank you for your time, sir. You have a good day.'

They left the pub, got on their horses, and headed back towards Waterford.

Robert sat at the bar and I went into the kitchen with Colleen. She really took a great risk lying for me.

'Thank you so much. You didn't have to....'

Colleen smiled, 'I did have to, or you'd be in chains on your way to Waterford.'

'But how did you know?'

She smiled quite proudly, 'I told you Mr. Ryan, I keep a mindful watch on the property. I heard you come in this morning and for a moment I thought someone was breaking in. I didn't recognise you. Then I saw you bringing in your saddle and watched you drag it all into your room. I knew you were up to no good.'

'The item I stole, was mine in the first place. I was merely taking it back.'

'No matter,' she said. 'You'd never last a week in prison. It's a miracle that you survived outside this long.'

'You've saved me again Colleen.'

'I think you were sent here from above. You've been good to my family, and helped us in more ways than you could know.'

'The feeling is mutual.'

'Mutual indeed, you might know we lease 20 acres of land and generally use most of it for potatoes. I listened to what you told me about the blight and what the experts said. We only planted half an acre of potatoes this year, and planted beets, and few other crops instead. All the potatoes rotted. It was a terrible smell. Every one of my neighbours lost their entire potato crop too. You're a godsend. You saved us a great loss.'

There was a strong connection I felt in that moment. Like a bond that family has, 'That's great!'

'You may be a curse to yourself,' she continued. 'But you've been a blessing to me and my family.'

'You've been a blessing to me as well.'

I reached over and gave her a hug. She almost teared up.

'I was at the farm today for supplies,' she said in a soft voice. 'Young Stephen said you never brought your horse by, and I saw you bringing your saddle in this morning. Please tell me you didn't kill another horse.'

My head dropped in shame, 'I did. She was carrying too heavy a load when I was running away from the IC. It was too much for her.'

She shook her head, 'You'll be making Harry a rich man at the rate you're going.'

I smiled and went back to the bar to join Robert.

Chapter 17

Hurry up and Wait

Robert ordered me a Guinness and I chugged back a mouthful. I looked at Stephen, 'Thanks for vouching for me.'

'It's no bother Mr. Ryan. I don't like the IC anyway. They ticketed me a few years back for serving alcohol during lent. Now I pay them to let me get away with it. They're corrupt through and through.'

'Thanks for covering for me, Robert. You do know it's a crime to lie to the IC?'

'I thought you would better be represented by someone in a suit. Don't take this the wrong way, but the Constabulary shows more deference to an Englishman in a suit, than an Irishman dressed informally.'

'No offence taken. It worked. I can't wait to show you my time machine. We should nurse a pint or two and pass some time, just to be certain they don't return.'

'I was thinking the same thing.'

We discussed a plan to charge my battery, and the many tools we'd need to reinvent. I would require chemicals and a lab to isolate argon gas. A vacuum tank, electricity, a pump, a generator, and a transformer to regulate the voltage. The list went on. Many of these things could be made in months with modern tools, but would take twice as long to build in this time.

Robert listened intensely.

'Here's my proposition. I'll require a large supply of materials, and a specialized crew to produce the argon gas and electricity needed to power my machine. I could finance all this myself and return to 21, but I'd rather include you and John.'

Robert smiled, 'You've already improved our lives tenfold.'

'I couldn't have gotten this far without your help. I'll be producing several inventions from the future to facilitate my vault back. I can draw up plans for all these things, and have our solicitor patent them. There will be several. You and John will be the richest men of this time.'

'What about your wealth? Perhaps you should consider staying here? You would have a much more substantial life than in 2021.'

'It would be financially prosperous to stay,' I said. 'With the wealth I've accumulated up to now, I could live out my life in relative comfort. Many of the people I've met, and the lives I've affected, have given me more fulfilment than I had in 21.'

'What about your social net,' he asked.

'Social network. There's no deep emotional connection. You can't smell it, taste it or feel it.'

I could hear the hope in his voice. 'Perhaps the future isn't for you anymore?'

'It has crossed my mind more than once. I've weighed out the pros and cons. I have greater purpose here, but I have friends and family in 21 that I miss.'

'You'll be missed here,' he sighed.

Life in 21 was about working, paying my bills, and saving for the future. Living in the past, especially in this time, was a test of survival. It invigorated me. I also wasn't as blind to the needs of others, as I was in 21.

'The amount of machinery and patentable ideas I will unleash will change the course of history. Several of these inventions won't be conceived until the end of this century, and beyond the 1900s. Some require electricity, motors, pumps, and refrigeration. There will be a century of discovery and innovation compressed into a few months. There's no telling how this will impact the future,' I said.

I wondered how these innovations would impact on the world I'd be returning to. I've seen it played out in movies, but the reality was, I would be releasing inventions that trickled onto the market decades after electricity was available. Producing electricity and several electric devices all at once would start a technological revolution. The electric refrigerator wasn't in people's homes until the 1930's. Mine would be created close to a century earlier.

'It sounds exciting,' Robert said. 'I will be living in a world that parallels yours by the time you are finished.'

'It won't be that big a leap, but it will bring Ireland and the world decades ahead.'

Robert was excited by the idea of bringing the future to his time. The money for him was secondary as we both were doing extremely well. I was going to have my share of the royalties from all the new inventions, put in Samuel and Eliza's name. I would retain the royalties from the zipper and sewing machine, to set up my sustainable farm.

I looked at Robert, 'So, shall we have a look at this thing?'

We headed to my room. Robert's eyes were fixated on the machine. 'How does it propel you?'

'It breaks you down into atoms, then transports you years into the past.'

'Unfathomable! The atom actually exists?' he asked.

'Yes. It's been proven for some time now. They've even photographed it.'

I showed him the keyboard and screen, took my knife, and unscrewed the back panel exposing the electronics. I was pleased to see it hadn't been opened or tampered with. I can only guess Phillip hadn't invented the Phillips screw or screw driver yet.

Robert gazed at the components, the gold of the electronics, and all its parts. 'This is more intricate than I could have imagined. How does one advance to this level of expertise?'

'Wait until I power it up.'

Robert was so excited to see this modern technology, he could barely contain himself. He was mesmerized, 'We have to bring your plan to John and get started right away!'

I felt Robert always retained a bit of doubt about my time travel. Not out of a lack of trust, but more out of a healthy skepticism. Having now seen my time machine and its components had erased any fragment of doubt.

John was spellbound when we approached him with the plans. 'You had all these ideas in your head all this time. Why didn't you mention them sooner?'

'Well John, my focus was on the sewing machines and zippers, but now I'd like to move on this.'

'We can use the workshop,' he said excitedly. 'When can you start?'

'I'll use the drawing table in the office at the linen factory to draft up the plans for the generator. Garth is working on some of the components already. I could have the generator plans completed in a few days, and our solicitor can file for the patent.'

'You're mind never stops,' John said with a smile.

'I should go and get some rest. It's been a busy couple of days.'

Sleep came quickly.

I awoke before sunrise energized, and headed to the office. Audrey arrived, peeked in, and greeted me. She seemed transformed. Confident.

Sitting in front of a blank piece of paper, I searched my memory and visualized each component. It was nice to have a proper drawing table, ruler, compass, and eraser. The humming of the sewing machines put me in a trance. I was incredibly focused and worked until sunset. One day led to the next and my routine continued. The generator plans were finally complete. I traced out a carbon copy for Garth, and passed the original on to our solicitor.

A smaller generator was needed for the chemistry lab at Trinity, in Dublin. Something that could be powered by a bicycle to recharge batteries. Battery power would be my primary source of electricity there.

Robert had told me salt water batteries existed in this time. They weren't rechargeable, and had no practical use except for simple science experiments. I would need to build lead acid batteries to store the energy I would generate at Trinity college. My time machine used a high voltage lithium battery. I had no plans of carting it back and forth to Dublin, it would be far too risky. If it was lost or damaged, I'd never be able to build a replacement. 1846 has only 58 elements, and lithium or cadmium would not be easily attainable. I needed so many things and yet wasn't sure if they existed in this time. If they didn't exist, they had to be built. My list of needs grew, exponentially.

Robert dropped in, 'How's it going?'

'Great! I just finished drawing up the plans for a lead acid battery. It can be recharged by using a small generator powered by a bicycle.'

'What's a bicycle?'

'A bicycle? You're kidding? I thought bicycles were two hundred years old.'

I sketched out a bicycle on a sheet of paper as Robert looked on. 'A hobby horse,' he insisted, then leaned over my shoulder, drew pedals on the front wheel and erased the drive chain. It resembled a child's tricycle. You pedalled the front wheel to move.

I rolled my eyes, 'I'm going to have another patent for you.'

'Have you read the paper?' he asked.

'No, not in weeks.'

'Sir Robert Peel has resigned. Just as you predicted.'

'It wasn't really a prediction. It's history.'

Robert grinned as he realized it was merely a historical fact.

My focus was on what I would need to bring to the lab in Dublin. A vacuum tank, a pump, several small fittings, cooling tanks, and a bicycle. Actually, half a bicycle. The drive chain would propel the back wheel. The wheel would be attached to a belt that would drive a small generator, and in turn generate my lead acid batteries. The acid would come from the lab at Trinity. The lessons I learned in chemistry class bored me when I was younger. They had taught us how to use a fractional distillation apparatus to produce nitrogen. At the time I thought, I would never need to make my own nitrogen. If I ever needed it, I could simply buy it. Who knew? Not simple at all. I would be using the same process to produce my argon gas.

Robert checked through my list of items and circled the items that existed, then left. I continued drawing. My task was not as difficult as I had imagined. Drawing up plans for machines that were already invented was surprisingly easy. These ideas took their inventors years to test and develop, as they used trial and error to achieve a point of discovery. I was simply copying from memory a functioning machine. I had made a few generators at the farm in 21, assembling components from a salvage yard to produce them. Now, I would need to actually build these components, then assemble them. Fortunately, I had a crew of 18 men to produce each part. My focus now, was to construct the machines I would need for Trinity, to produce the argon gas. Upon my return I would build a large generator and fix my time machine.

By the end of September, I had several patents pending and all the components cast. Now we would need to assemble them. I was so consumed with my work I failed to notice the collapse of Ireland around me. The blight had destroyed hundreds of potato crops over the summer, and hundreds more would not see a harvest in the coming weeks. Families left or perished, and dozens of English farm owners were selling.

Our solicitor was going to search and purchase a large farm on my behalf, while I worked on my stolen inventions. There was no time to finish everything I wanted to accomplish before I returned to 21. Suddenly, I wasn't in such a hurry to leave the past behind.

Chapter 18

Building for the Future

Weeks of drawing plagiarised inventions, would lead me from this time back to my own. I drew up plans for an electric sewing machine, even though I have yet to produce a usable electrical source.

Robert had established contact with his chemistry professor from Trinity college. He was intrigued by the discoveries I was to usher in, and the tools I would provide to do it. First, I had to assemble the parts that Garth had produced; everything I would need for the Trinity laboratory. The excitement was overwhelming. The small generator was the first piece to put together. I schooled Robert, Matt and his team on the function and placement of each part. It was important they understood how it worked, so they could build and repair copies of it when I was gone. A collection of copper, brass, iron, and magnets. It was a small device about the size of a large wine bottle. We spent days assembling it, taking it apart to retool it and putting it back together again, until all the parts moved smoothly. The half bicycle took us a couple of hours to piece together and attach to the generator. Matt began pedalling to produce power. We had no electrical devices to test it on. I certainly wasn't going to risk my time machine, or expose it to curious eyes. It didn't have the capacity to charge my lithium battery anyway. Instead, we were going to have a simple spark test. I had taken two of the wires attached to the generator. They were insulated in a resin mixture, and exposed at the ends. The positive and negative wires touched briefly and ignited a blue spark. Everyone was astonished with what they were witnessing. The birth of electricity. I struck the wires together again and again. It was incredible to see the sense of awe on all their faces.

Robert and I began assembling the parts for the pump and vacuum. Matt and his team attached various fittings to a number of pressure tanks; and a refrigeration unit. A few more days of assembling, disassembling, and retooling until, everything moved efficiently.

We were now ready to test the pump and the vacuum. It was an exciting time. They were about to witness a technological first, that wasn't supposed to happen for decades. Electricity in my time went through a series of baby steps in its infancy. We were taking it from birth to adulthood, in one step. I hooked up the vacuum to the power supply, and readied the switch. Matt sent one of his workers to fetch John, and had another one of his workers pedal the half bicycle. When John arrived, I threw the switch. It sputtered and thumped, as the pedalling continued. The excitement was boiling over. They were cheering and clapping. It was something I had witnessed before, yet for them it was like witnessing the first flight by the Wright brothers. Total bliss. The energy in the room was electric. The pump worked just as well. It was a great test. I had several lead acid batteries made for the laboratory in Dublin. Minus the acid. We would need these to run the vacuum and pump continually to produce the argon gas. The generator would be used to recharge the batteries as they depleted. I now had everything I needed. The rest would come from the lab. I arranged to have two men from the factory crate and deliver all the devices, and the batteries, to the laboratory in Dublin.

Now, I had the uncomfortable task of purchasing another horse from Harry Murphy. I went home, grabbed my saddle, and prepared for the walk of shame.

Harry greeted me with a smile.

'I'm going to need another horse,' I said in a timid voice.

'Stephen mentioned you might be in the market for one,' he said with a grin. 'Doing some more charity work?'

'Not exactly. I can only hope, the horse didn't go to waste.'

'You're going to make me a rich man, Mr. Ryan,' he said as we walked amongst the horses. 'I have to thank you for your advice on my potato crop this year, I normally plant 5 acres. It's an easy crop. I went with cabbage and beets instead, and I'm lucky I did. Every one of my neighbours lost their potato crops. I warned them all.'

'I'm glad it worked out for you. Sometimes it pays to listen to the experts, they're predicting the same thing next year too.'

I was happy I was able to change the course of history for a few people. I wish I could have spread the word to the rest of Ireland. Harry picked a beautiful black mare. He took my saddle from my shoulder and buckled it on her. She was fast and strong, and seemed to have a spirit about her.

'I'll take her,' I said.

As I handed Harry the money, he looked me in the eye, 'You may want to give her a name. It could help with her longevity.'

He had a point. It did work for Oprah. I grinned and headed home to pack for the ride to Dublin, then went to the pub for a pint and a meal.

Stephen greeted me, 'How are you doing today, Mr. Ryan?'

'Fine. I'm getting ready to ride to Dublin, so I bought another horse from your brother.'

He smiled, 'Third times a charm. You'll need to be extra diligent when you get there. I've been hearing stories about crowds, and a level of desperation that'll push a man to do ungodly things.'

'Thanks for the heads up.'

That was good to know. This year's crop failure was the start of Black 47. The worst of the famine was on its way. I took my beer to a table and ordered a meal. As I was finishing up, Stephen walked over with a bar rag. It gave off a heavy thump as he put it on the table, 'Take this with you,' he said. 'It might help you out of a situation. There's only one shot in the barrel.' It was the pistol he had taken from Samuel's thug.

'Thanks Stephen, I'll get it back to you when I return.'

Colleen cleared my dishes and put a pillow case on the table, 'There's some food in here for your trip Mr. Ryan. Stay away from trouble.' The mothering touch of Colleen was something I would miss.

I was up before sunrise and headed to Garth's shop to pick up my argon tank. He replaced the valve handle. I didn't want to ship it out with the rest of the supplies. This tank was part of my lifeline home, much like a scuba tank for a diver.

It only took a short ride to reveal the fallout from this year's crop failure. The farmers not yet stricken by blight were guarding their fields. I saw acres of barren land, with the wretched perfume fouling the air. A man wandered out to a field with beehives. He removed the roof of a hive, grabbed a frame of honey, and began eating it. He was a hundred metres away but I could see the madness in his eyes as he ate the comb, barely swatting the bees as they covered his face and hands. The sting of hunger was much worse than that of an angry colony. There were no bounds to what starvation would drive a person to do.

Crowds of people were lumbering towards Dublin. The bodies of the dead laid by the roadside. Their families were too weak to bury them. The physical and emotional toll from this would last for generations. I rode on.

The cities I had passed, nearer to Dublin were crowded. There was a much larger police presence. The Irish Constabulary were bold and relentless. When I reached Dublin, I could hear the songs of desperation. It was louder with an unfamiliar smell, something history books never spoke of. It felt strange to witness the unique odour of a grieved nation.

When I reached Trinity college, there was a police officer at the entrance. He directed me to the stables, and escorted me to the office. The secretary greeted me.

'I'm looking for a Professor Derek Belley? He's expecting me.'

She looked down at a notebook on her desk then back to me, 'You must be Mr. Ryan McCullough.'

'Yes.'

'I can get someone to take you to the lab,' she said.

'Is it still upstairs to the left?'

'Yes.'

'I'll find it on my own. Thank you.'

A very curious feeling came over me, walking through the hallway of my old college. It had a strange familiarity although it looked much different. As I peered into the laboratory, it reminded me of something from an old science fiction movie with beakers, test tubes, and whale oil burners. There was a class of a dozen students and a redheaded professor with a goatee. I knocked on the open door.

The professor glanced up, 'Can I help you?'

I stood with my argon tank in my hand and my saddle bags over my shoulder, 'I'm Ryan McCullough, the man Robert Feeney, contacted you about.'

He approached me with a smile. He had a pleasant way about him. A man that had obviously found his true calling, 'I was expecting someone older. Come in.' He shook my hand, 'I'm Doctor Derek Belley,' he said with a thick Scottish accent.

'Pleased to meet you Dr. Belley.'

'Call me Derek.'

'Well Derek, I have some exciting technology and discoveries I'd like to introduce. I spoke so fast I'm sure he could barely understand me.'

'Robert mentioned you had some novel ideas. I've been anticipating your arrival since I received his letters. He hinted that you have a process to isolate argon gas.'

'Yes,' I said. 'Nitrogen too. My main goal is to fill this tank here with argon.' I lifted the tank I was carrying. It was about twice the size of a 2-litre bottle. 'I also have a crate of apparatus arriving. Hopefully, by tomorrow. There's some cutting-edge equipment that I'm sure you've never seen before.'

'What will we be cutting?' he asked.

I smiled, 'We'll be working with some very innovative equipment.'

His green eyes glowed, 'This all sounds grand,' he said as he noticed my worn demeanour. 'I've set you up with accommodation near the institution. We should get you settled.' He instructed one of his senior students to take over the class. 'Oh! I almost forgot.' He handed me two jars. 'This is the chromium and carbon you asked for.' Two of the ingredients Garth was going to need for the stainless steel.

'Thanks so much,' I said. 'We can leave it here until tomorrow. I'll send it back with the boys that bring my equipment.'

Derek set me up in a house that accommodated new teachers. It was a showroom of antiques, but they were barely a few years old. The fabrics were bright and colourful, unlike the faded antiques of my time. They even had indoor plumbing.

'I hope this is suitable?' he said as he handed me the key.

'It's perfect. What about my horse?'

'You can leave it at the stable, they'll tend to it for you.'

What a great place. I unpacked my saddle bags, and walked along College Green. It was an unusual display of normal city life, with waves of stricken people wandering towards the Dublin docks. There were begging hands everywhere, occasionally being driven off by the Irish Constabulary. I wandered into a market; bought supplies I'd need for the next few days; along with a sack of apples. On my way back to the house, I set apples on top of fences, stone walls, and benches. I made sure I was discrete so I wouldn't clash with a crowd, eventually emptying my sack. I returned without incident, then soaked in the tub and slept.

Derek greeted me at the lab, 'Good morning, sir,' he said with a smile. 'Did you sleep well?'

'Very well. I hope that delivery comes early. I'm anxious to start. They left before I did, but I came by horse.'

Derek examined my tank, 'Do you think it will be possible to contain argon?'

'Absolutely. This tank was full of it last year.'

'What will you require?'

'We'll need ammonium chloride, and a nitrate to start.'

'We have everything right here,' he replied as he opened a large cabinet.

'Do you have any sulphuric acid?'

'I do. It was on the list, in Robert's letter. I have 6 gallons of it.'

'Great! We'll need it for the batteries. Have you worked with electricity before?' I barely took a breath between sentences. I was just so eager to start.

'Oh yes,' he replied. 'We have batteries here.' He reached into a cupboard and pulled out a small box. 'This is based on Alexander Volta's design. I made it with my students.'

'These batteries will need to be charged continually. I've built a generator that will require pedalling for several hours each day. I hope your students are ready for some exercise.'

'I like teaching hands on. It's all part of the discovery. Recharging batteries! How exciting.'

'Yes. Twelve volts.'

'Twelve volts?' We've never achieved such high voltage here at the lab.'

'We'll pair off the batteries in series circuit and use 24 volts,' I said.

I knew the salt water batteries were more of a novelty and had a low voltage. Robert told me about an electric motor they used when he was in college. It hooked up to a salt water battery and spun in circles. It consisted of a wire that was positioned between magnets and pivoted on a needle. It lacked any horse power that conventional motors possessed but was an exciting innovation for this generation.

Derek was receptive. All this was new and exciting, and some of my terminology was lost on him.

When his students arrived I addressed the class, 'This is going to be a great week of discovery. You'll be the first people to witness this technology. We'll be working with electricity and making scientific history.'

The students clapped and talked amongst themselves. Derek and I began setting up the equipment. He gathered the ammonium chloride and sodium nitrate we would need. The process involved heating it and capturing the gas in a fractional distillation apparatus, along with the vacuum when it arrived. From there it would pass through a series of tanks, followed by a heating and cooling process, gradually separating the gases. Nitrogen would be captured first for our refrigeration unit. We would then heat up magnesium it would also produce nitrogen. Argon was essentially the waste product of this process.

My men arrived with the crated goods. I gave them the carbon, chromium, and the formula for stainless steel to bring back to Garth.

The students helped me unpack the crates and fill the batteries with sulphuric acid. I connected the half bicycle to the generator, then had a student pedal. I touched the positive and negative wires together and the spark was followed by a gasp from everyone. It was a simple thing to me, but other worldly to the students. The excitement was contagious. Each battery was attached to the generator one at a time and charged by a pedalling student. It was a fun exercise... and exercise. For the remainder of the day the students took turns charging my 8 batteries.

Two days passed with the students pedalling continually. I set up a pair of batteries in series circuit explaining the significance as I did, and how it doubled the voltage.

Now we were ready. First, I began heating copper and ammonia to create nitrogen. Its off gas was filtered through a fractional distillation apparatus, then through a series of tanks separating the CO_2 and oxygen and other impurities. The vacuum would provide a lower atmospheric pressure to help the process. The gas would be compressed using the pump and the apparatus I had built. By the end of the third day, we had a small tank of liquid nitrogen, and a refrigeration unit ready to test. The classroom went silent. Everyone stood still as I hooked it up to the batteries and flicked the switch. It was chilling almost instantly. Watching the astonishment on their faces was incredible. The first electric freezer. This was not a simple light bulb. We were skipping over the stages of electrical development, and taking it decades ahead in a single step. The energy usage was immense. We switched out the batteries as they depleted, and continued regenerating the dead ones. The waterwheel back at the mill would provide a continual source of energy when I hooked it up to the larger generator.

The smaller generator, half bicycle, and acid batteries, were the only way I could create a portable electrical supply for the Trinity lab. Having accomplished this much in a few days was invigorating. Teaching the next generation these processes, would ensure the continuation of this technology, when I was gone. I pondered... how different 21 might be when I returned.

Derek and I spoke alone at the end of the day. He was overflowing with excitement, 'We need to document these findings for history, Ryan. You'll be renowned in the world of chemistry.'

'I don't need recognition for any of these findings. I have patents pending on all the apparatus, I'll do well by this. I'm just here for a tank of gas.'

'This is important and should be noted,' he insisted.

'I agree. It needs to be documented. I just don't want credit for this. We did it together. I would rather not be mentioned. It'll be good for you, and Trinity as well.'

'It wouldn't be right, Ryan.'

'Why?' We made the discovery together. It just happened to be with my apparatus.'

After a long discussion he agreed. He learned how it was done and would be able to duplicate the process on his own. His students would also be able to use the equipment for future discoveries. There was no need for me to be remembered in history. I really didn't deserve recognition for another stolen innovation.

Each morning was loud and exciting. The students couldn't wait to come to class, and arrived early. I instructed Derek on how to capture the argon gas, and he led the students through the process. It was similar to the method we used to capture the nitrogen. We spent days, refining, and compressing my elusive gas.

Derek and I discussed several experiments. He was curious and my answers were evasive. How could I tell him I acquired all my knowledge in this lab? I constantly changed the topic of my past, and Robert was wise not to mention that I attended Trinity. We discussed several useful experiments he could now pursue. He was thrilled to have new tools to take him into the future and I was thrilled to have the argon gas that would take me there. We could have continued our discussion for days but I had to get back, and needed to make a stop along the way. With my argon tank full, a new era of discovery was unleashed.

Chapter 19

Family Routes

At first light I was up, retrieved my horse, and was on the train, ready to be reunited with my 3rd great grandparents. There was so much to be thankful for, and I was excited to share the good news.

Once I left Drogheda Station, a new tragedy emerged. Groups of despairing people with barely the strength to walk, laying stone roads for the Public Works project. History had recorded the brutality of this scheme. Enslaving the weak and frail, so they could earn enough to eat. Most of them shoeless and dressed in rags, would likely perish before winter set in. The pain I witnessed was always more ruthless, than history had interpreted. My elation crashed, as I retraced my route back to Meeting Street.

I walked my horse down the alley to Samuel's shop in the rear.

'Hello!' I yelled. 'Hello.'

Samuel poked his head out of the shop, then squinted, 'Is that you Ryan?... Oh, good to see you.'

He gave me a hug, took the reins from my horse, and caressed his saddle, 'The saddle's a perfect fit,'

'Yes, it was made for her.'

'Well, let's get this off her and see Eliza and Joseph.' He unbuckled the saddle, noticed the blood stain but didn't say a word about it. 'Let's go inside.'

'Eliza! Eliza! Look who's here!' Eliza came downstairs with young Joseph. He was walking and talking now.

'Good to see you,' she said as she touched my cheek with the back of her hand. 'I like the clean-shaven face. You look a lot like Samuel did when we were dating, before he grew his beard.' Her stomach was bulging. I smiled and stepped back.

'Another one on the way I see. You mentioned it in your letters, but I had no idea you were this far along.'

'Aye. We're sure to have a girl this time. She's not a kicker like young Joseph here was.'

I didn't dare tell her she was going to have another son. 'Will you be staying long this time?'

136

'I was hoping to spend the night.'

'That's just grand. You can stay as long as you please.'

I patted Joseph on the head as he ran past. It felt great to be around family.

'Have a seat,' Samuel said as he pulled out a bottle of whiskey from the kitchen cabinet, then poured 3 glasses.

That whiskey wasn't going to be good for their unborn child, but this was not the century for me to talk about it.

'We can't thank you enough for what you've done for us,' said Samuel. 'It's a blessing in these hard times.'

'You mentioned in your letters, that you bought this place,' I said excitedly as I looked around their kitchen, 'That's great news.'

'Tis. Who would have thought we could own a home? Our landlord lost so many tenants, he was glad to accept our terms. Your gift was put to good use.'

'Well, that's why I came to see you. I have more good news to share.' They both sat quietly at the table as I spoke, 'I've been inventing machines in Doonass, and patenting them. There are two other men who are partners in this venture. Friends of mine. Do you know how the patent system works?'

'No,' they answered, as they both shook their heads.

'Well, to put it simply, I draw up plans for an invention, file the idea through my lawyer, and if no one has a similar idea, I get a patent and rights to that invention.'

They listened as we sipped our whiskey.

'Once I have the patent, any company that wants to build a machine like mine, is required to pay me a royalty. A small percentage, for everyone they produce. This is how I've been making my money.'

'That's so interesting. So, nobody can use your ideas without paying?' Eliza asked.

'Exactly. I'm going to transfer these royalties to you and Samuel. My lawyer has drawn up legal documents.' I reached into my saddle bags and pulled out an envelope. They sat there in shock. 'I need for both of you to sign these documents, and any money made from my share of the royalties will be transferred to you.'

'Why are you doing this?' Samuel asked. 'Why aren't you keeping it for yourself?'

'I'm receiving money from the patents I hold already, so I have plenty of money coming in. It's more than enough for me to live off. All you have to do is sign these documents, and the money from my newest patents will go to you.'

'Why are you doing this for us?' Eliza asked. 'We knew nothing about you until recently, and you've changed our lives in the best of ways.'

'You are family, and I want to share my good fortune with you. I'll be leaving in the coming weeks and I won't be returning.'

'You won't be returning?' Joseph asked.

'This is all very unusual,' said Eliza.

We continued to go over the details. They signed the documents and Eliza put their copy away. They had so many questions, but all my answers were evasive.

We celebrated with a light meal and a lot of whiskey. I was really drunk. We all were. Eliza put Joseph to bed. When she returned, I decided to tell them the truth.

'I've been keeping a secret from you.'

'Well,' Samuel replied. 'You're entitled to your privacy.'

'It's not something that's easy to say.'

'Are you ill?' Eliza asked.

'No. I'm as healthy as an ox.'

'Then what could be so hard to speak of?' she asked.

This was it. The moment of truth.

'I am a closer relation than I led you to believe.'

Their eyes were locked on me with a serious stare.

'I'm your great, great, great grandson.'

They looked at me sternly, then they both broke out in laughter.

'I'm not kidding,' I said defiantly. 'I came from the future with a time machine I had built.'

They continued to laugh. This was not the response I was hoping for. It was probably a bad idea but I continued. 'Eliza. Your child is going to be a boy.'

She laughed, 'It's to be a girl.'

'You're going to have a son, and you're going to name him Samuel.' They both quieted down. 'Then you're going to have another son. I don't remember what his name is, but your fourth child is a girl, and her name is Madal... Matilda.'

They looked at each other silently, then back at me.

'How did you know her name?' asked Eliza. 'I just chose that name a few days ago. I told no one, but Samuel.'

'It's in our ancestry records. I know it's hard to conceive. Your youngest son will be born 10 years from now. You will name him George, and he's my great, great grandfather.'

They weren't laughing now.

'This is impossible. Only Jesus Christ, himself would be capable of such a feat, Samuel continued, 'It must be a magic trick. You read minds.'

'It's not magic. It's science and physics.'

'Stop this talk,' he said. 'You're drunk.'

'I am drunk, but it's the truth. George will have a few children, and one of his sons Joseph, is my great grandfather. Then Joseph names my grandfather George after his father, and my father is named George as well.'

'That would be over a hundred years in the future,' Samuel cried out.

'2021 to be exact.'

'2021!' he cried. 'No machine could do that. You're drunk man.'

'You may not believe me now, but you will in years to come. Those inventions I created. They were machines made by men years from now. I just copied them.'

Eliza looked at me with a sad expression. These people lived simple lives and perhaps it was out of their realm.

'You tell a good story Ryan,' she said.

Samuel went outside to the back stairs and took a piss. I looked at Eliza.

'I know this all sounds impossible, but I will tell you a few things about the future, that will prove what I'm saying is true. 1847 is going to be the worst part of the famine. It's going to get desperate.'

Samuel returned from the yard.

'This famine, lasts until 1852. It will kill a million people and a million more will emigrate to England, America and Canada.' They looked at me as if I was being ridiculous, and it must have sounded that way. 'There's going to be an Irish rebellion in 1848. To overthrow the British.'

'Now you're talking!' Samuel said in jest.

'They don't succeed,' I replied. 'Queen Victoria, visits Ireland in 1849.'

'That's just daft,' he said. 'She doesn't give a shite about Ireland.'

'We're going to drive in cars, without horses and airplanes will

139

fly us around the world.'

Samuel laughed, 'Fly us around the world.'

'We'll have 2 great wars in Europe. Canada and America will be involved. They'll use airplanes and drop bombs.'

'Wars!' cried Eliza.

'Yes. Millions of people will be killed.'

Eliza gasped.

'You need to stop now,' Samuel insisted. 'You're upsetting Eliza. I appreciate what you've done for us, but it doesn't give you the right to tell such terrible stories.' Picking up the almost empty bottle of whiskey, he put it in the cupboard. 'I think we've had enough. We should be sleeping this off.'

'You're right. I'm sorry. I'm going to call it a night.'

I went upstairs to my cot. I felt horrible. This all went sideways. My hope was, they would embrace the truth, and it would be a special moment. A connection. It was just sad and pitiful. Samuel and Eliza followed a few minutes later. I could hear them whispering and giggling, before I passed out.

I woke up feeling hung over and disappointed. Samuel had some tea on, and poured me a cup.

'I guess you're feeling it this morning,' he said with a grin.

I half smiled, 'I've felt worse.' The truth was, I felt terrible. This was the last time I was going to see them, and now they saw me as an absurd fool. I'd be leaving on a sour note.

I looked at Samuel, 'I'm sorry about yesterday.'

'It's already forgotten. We all get hit by the drink every now and then.'

Eliza came down with Joseph, poured herself a tea and started breakfast.

'I better get going,' I said.

'You'll need some food in you first,' she replied. 'I wouldn't want to send you off on an empty stomach.'

'I'm sorry about yesterday,' I said in a sombre voice.

'Ah,' she said. 'Tis nothing. I don't take a night of drink too seriously.'

I ate some eggs, and said goodbye for the last time. Eliza gave me a hug, and a sandwich wrapped in a napkin.

Joseph escorted me out back to get my horse. He buckled on my saddle and looked up at me.

'Next time you come, we'll see if we can buff that stain out,' he said, as he pointed to my saddle.

I shook his hand; he gave me a hug and a pat on the back.

'Don't be so hard on yourself,' he said. 'It's just a night of drink. There's no harm done.'

I left down the alley and out to Meeting Street. Then headed south to the train station.

Chapter 20

Feast

The visit with my Greats was devastating. Alone in the cattle car, I brooded and grumbled to my horse. She lacked the sympathetic face of Oprah. I named her 47, primarily because she was black, and I was depressed.

The fog was thick and grey when I arrived in Dublin. I kept reliving the moment I exposed my secret and could see Samuel and Eliza laughing. It was gut wrenching. Perhaps I was too drunk to really think it through. They played down the whole ordeal this morning, but deep down I knew our relationship was tarnished forever.

I trotted down the streets of Dublin with no real direction in mind. There was a man standing on the side of the road with an uncomfortable look on his face. I watched as he knelt and picked something up. It was rope. He tugged it tight and tripped my horse. I was thrown, and tucked and rolled as I hit the ground. A second man appeared, grabbed 47's reins and ran down the road, as the rope man followed. I sat stunned and panicked for a moment, then gave chase.

They had everything. My horse, my argon, chemicals for my IV canister, the signed documents. I was frantic and watched them turn down an alley. My blood was boiling, I was angry, yet frightened. I ran up to the side of the alley, summoned up the courage to pursue, then went in. It seemed empty, cloaked in fog and old crates. The contents of my saddle bags were on the ground. My argon tank was still attached to the saddle of my horse. Suddenly, I was grabbed from behind. One of the men held a knife to my neck. A second man appeared with my pistol in his waist band. He spoke inches away from my face. I could feel the heat of his breath. It smelled like blight as he spoke through his rotting teeth.

'You had to follow us,' he said. As his partner held me tight.

'I have money! Just take it and leave everything else!'

He pulled my pistol from his waist and cocked it.

'You're a fool, man,' he said with intense eyes. 'I have the pistol. I can have it all.'

I was enraged. There was no fear, just anger. I had nothing left to lose.

'You're the fool,' I said defiantly. 'It's not even loaded.'

He clenched his jaw and smacked the pistol against my head. It went off striking his partner. I could hear the bone in his arm shatter as the gun powder burned my neck. He fell back. The ringing in my ears did not dampen his screams. The gun man was shocked. I wrestled for the pistol, and I began hitting him in the face. His partner ran out of the alley, his arm gushing blood and dangling like a rag.

'You could've had the money!' I screamed. 'You could've had it!'

I released my passion on him with the worst brutality until he went limp. I thought I'd killed him. After scooping up my belongings into my saddle bags I mounted 47. The man on the ground rolled to his side and began coughing up blood as I rode off. An hour later I pulled off to the side of the road, and broke down crying. I scarcely took a breath, and sat in a field until my panic subsided. The events of the last couple of days were signs that it was time for me to go. I mounted my horse and continued my journey back to Doonass.

I'd acquired everything I set out for, yet felt empty. Blocking out my worries, I listened to myself breathe, until stillness cloaked my thoughts.

When morning came, I laid in bed for hours wallowing in self-pity. It was time to move on, I needed to return to my time.

Heading to the black smith shop, I regained my focus.

Garth greeted me with a smile, 'Hello Ryan. I finished your stainless-steel parts.'

'That was quick.'

'It was a labour of love. I was compelled. Such an incredible alloy.'

'Well, you now have the formula. I'll find out where the laboratory sourced the chromium, and get that information to you.'

'Thank you.'

I gathered the parts he completed, and headed to the linen factory. Robert was in the office. He was spending most of his time working on my new inventions, and less time at the sewing machine factory.

'Good morning. How did things go in Dublin?'

'Everything went well,' I said. 'I got everything I needed.'

'Is it in the sack?'

'No. This is from Garth. It's my stainless-steel parts. I thought they'd be safer here, when I assemble my time machine.'

'Absolutely,' he replied, as he opened a cabinet. 'Put them in here. By the way, Brett told me you took a sewing machine last week.'

'Yeah, I told you I was taking one. Is that a problem?

'No, of course not, but you asked for it months ago, before you found your time machine. Why would you need it now?'

'I gave it to Audrey.'

Robert was shocked, 'Why?'

'We both know the linen industry is going to collapse in the next year or two, and Feeney's Linens may die with it. Nobody is immune. I've been encouraging Audrey to plan for her future. To open her own tailor shop.'

'Why didn't you tell me?'

'I'm telling you now. I gave it to her before I left for Dublin.'

'You care too much about these people.'

'Come on now. You've mellowed in the last year. I thought you might feel good about this. Like the dresses.'

Robert didn't seem to know how to react. He had softened his stance with his employees, becoming less stringent and developing a bit of social character... although, it was often prompted by me. Feeney's Linens was still thriving, but it was eclipsed by the sewing machine and zipper profits, and he knew his future was secure.

'You're right. It's probably a good gesture, and I do appreciate the work she has done for us.'

'Good. I told her it was from both of us.' Robert smiled. He knew I was trying to encourage a change in his behaviour, as I had done throughout my time here.

'I'll give her my regards, when I see her,' he said.

My mood was still sombre from my recent experiences, and Robert could tell I wasn't feeling my best. Like a good friend, he could read me, and had a way of pulling me out of a funk, seeming to take pleasure in it.

'Are you well?' he asked.

'Yes. It's been a rough couple of days. I think the end of my time here is getting close. I just thought I'd be more excited.'

'Then stay,' he replied excitedly.

'I can't. I have to go back.' My emotions were all over the place. I was happy about returning to the safety of 2021, yet sad about leaving this extraordinary life I was living. I was experiencing an absurd sense of loss anticipating the future.

Robert shuffled some papers on his desk, 'I have good news.' he said, as he held a document in his hand. 'Our solicitor found you a farm. You just need to sign for it.'

'Where?'

Robert smiled, 'It's not far from here. Let's get a coach. I'll show you.'

We took a coach out of town, and pulled up to a barren piece of land divided by hedgerows, and blackened by blight. Wild grass partially covered the land, and would provide good grazing. It spread out over hundred acres, with 30 plots for farmers and their families. Each lot had a stone home with a burned-out thatch roof, and backed onto the River Shannon. It was perfect. Unfortunately, it was a property I'd never be able to enjoy. However, I felt confident it would ensure the survival of many. I had discussed the particulars with Robert, months ago. The farmers would pay a token fee. Ten percent of the market rate. They would be bound by contract to grow anything but potatoes, until 1853. This was to ensure no one had a failed crop. Robert would use the rents to pay the taxes, and the rest would be set aside for disaster relief. He would also manage my royalties from the sewing machines and zippers. The funds would finance the soup kitchen, along with a trust fund set up in Samuel and Eliza's name. We walked the property for an hour. I felt uplifted being able to make a small difference in these horrible times.

'What are your plans, when you return to 2021?'

Up until now, I hadn't thought much about my future in the future. I had lost so much in 21. My focus after my wife's death, was building the time machines. During my time here, I always had a task and a goal. A daily challenge.

'I thought I'd sell my time machine, it would be worth millions; but the more I think about it, the less sense it makes.'

'Your ideas have done you well here. Why not profit in your time too.'

'Those ideas weren't mine. The only invention I have is the time machine.'

'Then why should you not profit from it,' he said.

'It's not that simple. The kind of person that could afford this would have significant money and power. I'd use it to stop future wars, a person with that much power would use it to win them. It would be too dangerous to sell.'

'A man with power is a dangerous thing, but you'll need some financial security, when you return.'

'Yes. I'll have to start from scratch. I'm not sure how my meddling in this time is going to affect my future. If my family manages the wealth I leave them efficiently, I may end up inheriting my own wealth. How cool is that?'

We took the coach back to town. Robert dropped me off at the parish hall.

Father McGarry greeted me. He was helping the nuns feed a line of people.

'Hello father.'

'Hello Ryan. How are you today?'

'I'm well father, I'm here on a mission.'

'What would that be?' he asked.

'I'm looking for 30 families in need of a home.'

'Well, you can pick out anyone from this crowd here, they're all in need. What did you have in mind?'

'I'm looking for someone with leadership skills? I will need someone that speaks, both English and Irish, to help run this project.'

Father McGarry was intrigued by my housing scheme, and introduced me to a man named Peter. Peter had lost his wife and was raising two sons. I explained to him, he would not really oversee the community, he would just be the go-to guy. I would provide cheap housing, but there would be stipulations. Contracts would be drawn up, as a protection for the tenants in case something nefarious happened when I was gone. Every family would have a document proving their right to live in their home, and allowing it to be passed down for generations. To ensure their success, they would be bound to raise any crop other than potatoes, until 1853. The low rent would enable them to sell their crops, and build up enough savings to purchase their own plot or live out their lives with financial security.

The landlords charged enormous rents and most families worked the land all year just to pay it. My plan would break this cycle.

Peter was thrilled with the idea. Who wouldn't be? He was a man that had lost hope, and was offered a new lease on life. I picked out 20 men and women from the soup line. Peter translated my proposal. We agreed to meet in two weeks, to sign the contracts, giving them possession of their new homes. It was times like this I wished I was staying to see this through. I wasn't sure how long this idea could sustain itself without hands on management. My hope was, it would last indefinitely.

The days passed, and I worked with Robert and Matt's crew on the generator and transformer. It was slow, but methodical. I explained how and why it worked, as well as the dangers of electricity. They needed to know everything, so they could carry on this work when I was gone. Most of what I told them was written down for future reference. I built a small motor from parts we made for the pump, then modified one of our sewing machines. It was crucial I had an electrical appliance to test the generator. I didn't want to risk blowing up my battery when I recharged it. Our hard work came to end. The transformer was assembled, and the generator was nearing completion. It was about the size of a small car.

Two weeks had passed, and it was time to venture back to the parish hall. I had 30 contracts drawn up for my housing project. A few guys from Matt's team signed on, and a few seamstresses from Robert's linen factory as well. The remainder came from the soup line. Once all contracts had been signed, we agreed to meet at the farm the following morning.

It was an incredible sight. Two hundred people showed up carrying their possessions, or towing them behind in carts. The houses didn't even have roofs, but they were just happy to have a place to start a new life. I had come prepared. I put 2 shillings in each home to give the families a fresh start. A wagon over flowing with cabbage, onions, parsnips, and beets was unloaded on Peter's lot. Harry Murphy sold me a bull, and several of the men helped butcher and distribute the meat. Women gathered thatch for the roofs, while others built a fire and prepared a feast. Everyone pitched in. It was the first time I had seen so many people smile. Just before dusk, we all gathered. Sitting side by side, encompassing Peter's hedgerow, we all shared a meal. Although I didn't understand the Irish language, I did understand happiness. Everyone was singing, dancing, and playing music. This was the birth of a new community.

Chapter 21

Going forward

As my last days here ticked away, I reminisced about my time spent in our tragic past. It was difficult, but exciting. Dangerous, but invigorating. It was an experience that couldn't be rivalled. Defining moments were a regular occurrence, to witness history and become a part of it. I was living a privileged existence, only a time traveller could live. The appeal of returning to a normal life in 21 seemed strangely dull. My life here had purpose.

I spent time alone in Robert's office putting the final touches on my time machine. The primitive rebuild surpassed my expectations. The miles I had travelled, and the pain I endured, led me to these two simple tasks; charging my battery with the generator, and testing my machine. My progress was hindered by my own grandiose design. Scaling the generator up from my original plans added weeks to the build. Deep down I knew I was stalling and wasn't ready to vault back to 21.

On Sundays I'd ride out to my farm and revel at the progress. The roofs were all thatched. The fields were planted with winter cabbage and other hearty crops. They had chickens and sheep. A spark of light in these calamitous times. This would be my last visit to the farm before I returned to 21.

After weeks of assembly the generator was finally complete. It was installed in the mill. Matt attached a belt to the shaft of the water wheel. The copper, iron, and brass, glistened as it spun like a jet engine. It made a soft whirling sound as it turned. I plugged the electric sewing machine into the transformer, attached to the generator. Robert, Matt, and John stood quietly watching. I invited Audrey to witness the new technology she would be using. The staff in the mill stood motionless. I engaged the foot pedal on the sewing machine. The motor whined and turned, and the needle sputtered across a strip of fabric. Electricity was created, and a new age would follow. Clapping and cheering rang through the mill. It was an extraordinary event for anyone in this time to witness.

I retrieved my battery from Robert's office, plugged it into the transformer, and watched and paced until the green light illuminated. Carrying it back to Robert's office, I stowed it in the cabinet.

'Are you going to test it?' he asked.

'Later, when the factory is closed. I need to calm down. Do you want to go for a pint?'

'Most definitely.'

Stephen greeted us with a smile, 'Hello gentlemen,' he said, as he poured our beers. 'Your case of whiskey arrived Mr. Ryan. I put it in your room.'

Robert looked at me and smiled, 'Are you planning to tie one on before leave?'

'Parting gifts.'

We reminisced about our time together.

'Things will be particularly dull when you're gone,' Robert said.

My mood was sombre, 'I'm going to miss it here. I've become attached to so many exceptional people. Relationships here have a special bond that I've never experienced in 21. Don't get me wrong, I love my friends and family in my time. They would do anything for me. The difference is, 1846 is dangerous compared to 2021. My friendships here have kept me alive. It'll be difficult adjusting to a normal life again.'

'If you don't like it, you can always come back. I'll be managing all your affairs when you're gone.'

I never seriously considered returning before. I wasn't sure that I could. The whole thing was an accident in the first place. Trying to duplicate the exact date I arrived would be improbable. Even my directions were off. I was aiming to land in Limerick, not Clifden. My sheep landed near Ennis weeks earlier. There are so many variables involved, I doubt I could duplicate them with any accuracy. We finished our beers and headed back to Robert's office.

It was quiet and dark. I lit a lantern, cleared the desk, and pulled the time machine out of his cabinet. Once the battery was hooked up, I booted up the computer. The chime and light startled Robert.

'This is far more spectacular than you described,' he said, as he relished the glow of the screen.

'I haven't even done anything yet.' I needed to consider this was the first time he had witnessed electric light. I thought I'd start off with my photo file. Robert was fixed on the screen, completely enthralled. There were pictures of my car, vacation photos of the Caribbean, and airplanes. I even had pictures of outer space. Then I unleashed the video file. We watched clips of my late wife, music videos, and a movie with special effects.

He scarcely blinked as he stared at the screen. He was completely smitten, 'I had no idea the future would look like this. When you explained it to me, I pictured it differently. Everything seems so perfect.'

'That's the future, my friend. This is what I'm going back to.'

Suddenly the office door flew open. We were startled and nervous. It was John.

'What is this?'

I stammered, speechless for a moment, 'It's a time machine.'

He was shocked and amazed. Gravitating to the screen, his gaze was fused.

'I saw the strange glow from outside,' he said. 'This is spectacular! How does it keep time?'

'I'm from the future. I used this machine to transport me from the year 2021.' Doubtful, but intrigued, he listened attentively.

It was quite easy to convince him once he saw the pictures, and videos on the screen. I showed them my 3D design software. They were mesmerised by the keyboard, and my typing skills. John and Robert bombarded me with questions, and I spent hours answering; revealing as much about the future as I could.

'I'm leaving tomorrow.'

'You have to stay! At least build another machine like this before you go.' John said.

'I can't. There's only one of these. The complex parts for this won't be available for 170 years.'

He was disappointed to witness the technology of the future, then have it taken away. I demonstrated the functions and software on my computer. They found the calculator fascinating. I can't imagine how they would react, if I was able to search the web. It was getting late. I reluctantly powered down, but they continued to stare at the blank blackened screen.

At sun rise, I purchased some gifts, before heading to the linen factory. John and Robert were waiting eagerly, in the office. They couldn't wait to see me.

'I tied my horse out back, Robert. It's yours now.'

Setting a case of whiskey on the floor, I pulled two bottles, and handed them to John and Robert. I presented Robert with my yellow coat.

He took it and smiled, 'I'll wear it around my estate, or when I travel abroad.' He knew he couldn't wear it in town, in case Samuel spotted it.

I reached in my wallet and handed John a fiver. 'What's this?' he asked.

'It's money, from my time.'

He stared at the complex design and colour, and grinned.

Again, they bombarded with endless questions about the future, as I filled my IV tank with electrolytes and chemicals, readying it for my vault.

'Can we see one of those videos again?' John asked.

'No problem. There's a great music video I think you'll enjoy.' I powered it up.

They both gasped as it chimed and glowed.

Sinead O'Connor was singing "Skibbereen," a ballad about the famine. They were sombre and curious.

'Do all the women shave their heads in your time?' John asked.

I chuckled, 'No. They're free to carry themselves any way they please.'

The special effects in the videos astonished them, and they struggled to differentiate the real from the CG. John and Robert were like children watching a cartoon... which I also showed them. I was in and out of the office distributing whiskey to Matt and his crew, and gifts to Audrey and the seamstresses. It was pleasant and somewhat festive.

Returning to the office, I interrupted their trance, 'OK guys, we should get some lunch. I need to recharge this battery.' They both pouted like toddlers, as I powered down my time machine and took the battery next door to the mill.

It was a strange way to spend my last day. Then again, how does one spend his day before he vaults himself 175 years into the future. Our conversation continued at the pub as we ate. I didn't know how to say goodbye to the Murphys. I left John and Robert at the bar, and went to my room to retrieve my saddle bags. I placed a letter and some gifts on the table, then gave my room a sad goodbye.

We sat and drank and talked for hours, as I interacted with Colleen, Stephen, and Mary, for the last time. Inside, my heart was broken as I held back the emotions I was feeling. We finished our drinks as daylight faded. Mary lit the lanterns, and this was our cue to leave. I took in the pub one last time, and left.

Robert waited in the office while John and I went to retrieve my battery. The workers were finishing their shift.

John looked at me as I unplugged it,' Don't go anywhere until I return.'

I smiled, 'Don't worry. I don't intend to set up until everyone has left.'

In Roberts office, I attached the battery. He looked at me with a sad expression. 'This is getting real,' he said with a smirk, as he mimicked one of my colloquial terms.

'Very real. I'm really going to miss you.'

'I'll be missing you too my friend. I hope your future is fruitful.'

'It won't be too difficult.' Riffling through my saddle bags, I pulled out 2 bottles of whiskey and a jar of honey.

'I see you're bringing back the necessities. Do they not have honey in your time?'

I looked at him as I held up the jar, 'Not as pure as this.' I dumped a pillow case with over 300 gold coins and some trinkets, on the floor.

Robert shook his head and smiled, 'Gold, that should ensure you some prosperity.'

'It's my insurance policy in case my relatives squander my inheritance.'

John returned, and I heard Audrey lock the front door.

'This is it,' I said.

Robert helped me carry the time machine into the factory, and John brought my saddle bags. We placed the time machine on a table.

I gave them both a hug, 'Thank you for everything you've done for me. I'm really going to miss you guys.'

We were all quite subdued. I powered it up, and typed in my coordinates. Robert helped me tie it to my back. I inserted the intravenous line and probe into my wrist. John stepped forward and straddled my saddle bags over my shoulder.

'Stay a few yards back guys,' I shouted, as I opened the valve to my argon tank. I pushed the button, said my final goodbye, and watched as the blue flash ignited. I woke up to daylight.

I was definitely back in my time. There was a tarmac road and lamp posts with wires. I watched from a field, as cars drove by.

Wiggling out of the ropes, I lugged my machine to a small derelict shed, hid it under some debris and carried my saddle bags out. Seeing buildings in the distance, I walked in that direction. Consumed by joy, I danced, and sang.

A sign read, Brandon Cork; a couple of hours from my home in Kerry. I wanted to call my mother, my family, everyone.

I went into a cell phone store. It was strangely different. I could only assume the technology I had introduced, put us decades ahead from when I had left. There were phones that strapped to your wrist and projected a keypad on your hand, wireless headsets you could wear like earrings. The choices were endless. I selected a classic design. It was much thinner than my Apple, and it had some flex. When it came time to pay, I handed the clerk my credit card.

'What's this?' he asked.

'It's my credit card.'

He chuckled, 'Are you pranking me?'

I wasn't sure what he was talking about, 'I just want to pay for the phone.'

He shook his head, 'We don't accept antique cards here.'

'It's not an antique, look at the date.' Although I was gone for over a year... I had arrived back to my own time...it should be as if no time had passed.

'My dad had one of these 20 years ago,' he replied. 'Unless you have cash or a credit chip I can scan, I can't give you the phone.'

Credit chip? Wow! I needed a phone and I only had €200 in cash. I reached into my saddle bags, pulled out my pillow case of gold coins and handed one to the clerk.

'This is worth more than the phone,' I said.

'I can't take this. It has to be cash. There's a pawn shop down the road, they buy and sell old coins.'

'Hold my phone. I'll right be back.'

The man at the pawn shop examined my coin with cotton gloves, while commenting on its quality.

'How much is it worth?' I asked.

He pulled out a book, flipped through the pages, and looked up, 'I can give you €2800 for it.'

'Great! I have over 300.'

'Three hundred!' he shouted. 'I only have enough cash for one. Let me make some calls and get back to you about the other coins.'

'I'll take the €2800 for now.'

I took his money and paid for my phone. I powered it up and stared at it. Feck. I couldn't remember anyone's number.

I needed to rent a car, but didn't have a credit card that worked. It was hard to believe I was now back in my time, and facing the same dilemma I had in 45.

There was only one option. I returned to the pawn shop. 'I need to borrow a car. My credit card doesn't work. I'll give you a €1000 cash if you lend me yours for a day.'

He smiled and raised his brow, 'I'd take that deal, but how do I know you'll return it, or bring it back in one piece?'

'Ok, here's what I can do. Fill out a pawn receipt for €16,800. I will leave you 6 gold coins as collateral. You'll still get €1000 cash, and if I bring it back damaged you can hold my coins until I pay up.'

'Alright. Sounds good to me. Let me fill out a receipt and have you sign it.'

I gave him 6 coins, signed the receipt and he handed me a ring. 'What am I supposed to do with this?'

'That'll get you in my car. It's the green one in the back.'

This new technology was going to be a learning curve.

We walked me out back, and he showed me how the ring unlocked the door and started the car.

'Where are you going?' I gave him the Eircode.

He pushed a button on the dashboard. 'Take me to P51K1W5. Ok you're ready to go.'

It was self-driving. I was on my way.

We passed the shed by the field. 'Stop!' I got out and loaded my time machine in the back.

As the car drove on, I anticipated seeing my mother after more than a year. It was a strange feeling. Time was relative. For her it would be as if I never left. The car stopped in front of her house. I ran up and tried to open the door. It was locked. A man opened it, and looked at me sternly.

'What the hell do you want?'

'My mother,' I replied.

He laughed, then yelled, 'Get the hell off my property!' slamming the door in my face.

I wasn't sure what to think. Did my interactions in the past somehow lead to my mother's premature death, like in the movies?

I continued to my brother's house, my sister's house... neither existed. It was terrible. Did I kill off my family? What have I done! I sat in the car and cried. There was no scientific explanation for this. I needed to collect myself. I needed to get home and continued on.

When I arrived, there was no building there. I could see my neighbour's house but mine was gone! What else had I changed?

Now I was back in my time, with no one to share it with. No home! No family! No idea what I was going to do.

I'll go to Doonass, I said aloud. 'Please push the command button before you log your directions,' the car replied.

The long drive gave me a chance to collect myself.

The mill was now a field. All that remained, were remnants of crumbled stone. Feeney's Linens, was still standing, but it was a decaying shell. A strange feeling overcame me as I walked into the vacant structure. I was just here a few hours ago, yet well over a century had passed. Standing in the exact spot I had just vaulted from, I felt empty. Why did I leave?

I continued through town, reminiscing about the buildings that had been replaced with concrete and glass. Every so often an original structure appeared, and I'd remember the shops, and the faces of the keepers.

I stopped in front of Murphy's pub. It wasn't called Murphy's any longer, but it was still functioning as a pub. I went in. The place felt hollow without Stephen greeting me, or Mary and Colleen.

It still maintained a rustic feel, the floor tiles were worn and the furniture was old. I walked past the kitchen. There was now an indoor bathroom at the end of the hall. The back door led out to a patio, full of people with a view of the River Shannon. My living quarters were gone, and so was the outhouse. Not seeing my room, gave me an empty feeling. I felt gutted and alone. My present was empty, now my past was gone as well. I'd lost them both.

The bartender served me a cold Guinness. He lacked the warmth and personality, Stephen possessed. I looked around, picturing the way it used to be. The fireplace was gone, replaced by heating panels. A television stood where a mirror used to be. A glass case hung on the wall. Inside was my dart board. Mounted beneath was a small plaque reading: "This is believed to be the very first dartboard. 1845." I smiled. For a moment, it felt like I was back in 45 enjoying a pint at Murphy's. Sadly, that moment passed. I drank up, got back in the car, and headed towards the farm I had purchased. The whole thing was bizarre. Riding in a self-driving car and touring my past.

As I approached the farm, the passage of time had reshaped it. The thirty stone houses were gone, although there were derelict remnants of a few still visible. Hedgerows were knocked down, transforming it into 8 large lots, each with a home appearing only decades old. I was compelled to stop at the house built on Peter's old lot. It seemed familiar. I walked up and rang the doorbell. My mum answered. How was this even possible? My heart was pounding. I hugged and squeezed her so tight.

She laughed, 'What's got into you?'

'I'm so happy to see you!' I cried.

'You see me every day. What did you do to your hair?'

I couldn't digest what was happening. In my mind, this was the house I grew up in. My memories were scrambled. I could only speculate, that my intrusion in my past, had somehow changed the past I had known. I remember spending my childhood here, but also in Kerry. My brother Randy was sitting on the sofa watching a match.

He waved from his seat, 'Hey bro.'

I gave him a hug, 'Great to see you!'

'What are you doing man?' he asked. 'Have you been drinking? Why are you dressed like that?'

My emotions were boiling over. I was confused, but happy. Suddenly I had regained everything that I had lost. My thoughts were scrambled between two realities. The memories I had growing up in Kerry, and the new ones of growing up here. Buying this farm had obviously changed the course of my family's migration. Instead of moving from Magherafelt to Kerry, they must have moved here. This was the only explanation I could fathom, although none of it made sense.

My brother glanced at me, then out the window, 'Why are you driving that green thing? Something wrong with your car?'

'I don't have a car.'

'What?' he asked, as he walked to the front door and opened it. He looked to the house next door, pointing to the car out front,

'What are you talking about? It's right there.'

I peered over his shoulder. My memories continued to scramble. I remembered that car, and that house. They were mine. It all felt like a dream. I was overwhelmed to see family, and so happy to see my Ma's face as she smiled.

'I was just going to make your brother a sandwich,' she said. 'Would you like one?'

'Absolutely! I would love one Ma.'

'Listen to you. You sound like you've just won a lottery.'

If only she knew. My heart was bursting with happiness.

I walked around the room, looking at old photos hanging on the wall. They were new memories for me, yet I could sense the photographs had been taken here. One picture stood out. Hundreds of people sitting on the hedgerow around our house.

'What's this pic of?' I asked Randy.

'What have you been smoking,' he replied. 'That's the annual hedge fest. You're sitting on the wall.'

I scrutinized the picture. I remembered being in it, but that was 20 years ago.

My mum came in with a sandwich, she put mine on the dining table, and gave Randy his on the sofa. I ate as I gazed around the room. All the furniture seemed familiar. The table, the buffet, the China cabinet. There it was, the brass kettle I had given to Eliza. I almost choked on my food. I plucked it from its glass cage, brought it back to the table, and admired it. My mum stared, as I polished it with my sleeve.

'Where did you get this?' I asked.

'Surely you've heard the story more than once,' she replied.

'I don't remember.'

'It was given to your great, great grandfather, by his mother Eliza. She was a strange eccentric woman. She gave him explicit instructions to pass it on to his youngest son, Joseph. She wrote a note for Joseph, to pass it down to his son George, your grandfather. He gave it to your father. She knew their names even before they were born. We used to joke that she had special powers.'

I was overwhelmed. Somehow, I knew she wanted it to get back to me. I had only written her once after my last visit, and she wrote me back, thanking me for everything. Neither of us mentioned the drunken night, I revealed my true self. It certainly soured our relationship. Although it happened 175 years ago, it was only a couple of months for me. Seeing this brass kettle now had lifted my spirits.

My mother leaned over and wiped a tear from my eye, 'Why are you crying?'

I wiped my eyes with my sleeve, 'I'm just happy. I'm just happy Ma. Did she say anything else?'

'No. That's all she said. Everything else is in the letter.'

I was stunned, 'What letter?'

'In the kettle.'

I opened the kettle and there it was. The letter. "To Ryan McCullough, open in 2021." I teased it gently from the envelope, then unfurled it.

It read:

Dear Ryan:

I always felt poorly about our last get together. I had written you dozens of times over the months and years, but never received a reply. I realized you probably went back. It wasn't that I doubted you, I just never thought it to be possible. Everything you told me that night, I wrote down in my diary. Everything you said was true. We both felt terrible we didn't take your words as truth. Samuel carried that regret the rest of his life. We both did. I'm a grandmother of 12 now. George is my youngest son, and he fathered 4 of my grandchildren. Joseph is his youngest. He will be getting the kettle from his father, and one day it will be back in your hands again.

I love you now, and I'll love you from heaven.

Your great, great, great granny Eliza.

I broke down in tears. My mother got up and hugged me, 'What's the matter dear?'

'This letter was for me,' I cried.

Randy came over and patted my shoulder, 'It's OK brother. You weren't even born yet. It's just a strange letter.'

I took a deep breath and collected myself. It was truly an amazing thing. It had come full circle. I sat there with a grin on my face, then looked at my Mum, 'You opened it. You opened the letter.'

'That letter was opened over a hundred years ago,' she said. 'Everyone in the family has read it for generations. I thought for sure you had read it. Your name's on the envelope. There's no harm reading it now, or three years from now.'

'Three years? Why 3 years?'

'Well, it says 2021 on the envelope.'

I had been living in the 1800s so long I hadn't noticed anything unusual when I came back, except for the technology. I sold my coin, bought my phone, and had a beer, and no one was wearing a mask.

'What year is this?'

Randy replied sarcastically, 'It's 2018 genius.'

I don't know how it happened. All the extra weight I was carrying must have sent me back a few years early.

I sprung out of my chair, gave my Mum a hug, and raced for the door.

'Where are you going?' she shouted.

'I have to find my wife.'

Randy shouted as I left, 'But you're not married.'

Big thanks.

I'd like to thank my Gorta book club who read each chapter. They shared their opinions, criticism, and encouraged me to write the next chapter.

Shane McCullough
Mirav Ozeri
Mickey Hegedus
Colleen Belley
Derek Belley
Jason McCullough
Stephen Small
Jennifer Bartolotti Small
Sarah James
Peter Gibson
Scott Shilling
Audrey McCullough
Vance McCullough
Gail O'Connor - McCullough
My brother Randy that never lived to see it.

Debra Bartolotti who helped me through the final polish.